PRAISE FOR *A BIRD ON EVERY TREE*

Bruneau's writing rarely calls attention to itself, but this is a bravura performance.... [A] close examination reveals every sentence to be carefully crafted, with an attention not only to sense and sound but character and place. As a result, every story feels unique and spontaneous, genuinely surprising.... This is no mere exercise in voice: this is a reflection of a writer utterly in touch with her stories—not only what they are, but how they are, overlooking nothing in her craft. Bruneau is a master. We should know this by now, but *A Bird on Every Tree* is a powerful reminder."
—starred review, **Quill & Quire**

"Each of Carol Bruneau's stories is not so much told as meticulously shaped with exacting and mesmerizing attention to every gorgeous detail. Bruneau submerges the reader entirely in the physical and emotional worlds she so vividly evokes."
—**Lynn Coady**, Giller Prize–winning author of *Hellgoing*

"This collection of short stories by one of Atlantic Canada's beloved storytellers is ambitious, eloquent, honest. A writer who crawls inside her characters and brings their hearts to the page."
—**Donna Morrissey**, award-winning author of *The Fortunate Brother*

"Carol Bruneau is the Mavis Gallant of the North Atlantic. Her diverse stories illuminate entire lives, each story as rich and deeply layered as a novel. Her narrative voice is an extraordinary blend of elegance and grit, the characters and their observations both pragmatic and elegiac. These are stories of a diverse range of people...all told with startling detail, lyrical prose, and uncanny insight into those moments which break us apart and those which hold us together."
—**Christy Ann Conlin**, author of *The Memento*

"A wide range of twelve beautiful and genuine stories, all connected through the considerable pull of Nova Scotia.... The tying knot pulsing through these stories seems to be that you can leave, but you will still be tethered to Nova Scotia. Perhaps by some long invisible salt chain, a guiding light reminding you of where you come from."
—**Atlantic Books Today**

"In these dozen bittersweet tales, Carol Bruneau writes persuasively and engagingly about love, longing, and loss.... a fine collection that is grounded in the real world and profoundly human."
–**Ian Colford**, author of *Perfect World*

"The stories in *A Bird on Every Tree* are decidedly larger than the few pages they inhabit.... Ms. Bruneau writes with a graceful precision and has a deftness with words and their cadences, their implications and meanings."
–**The Miramichi Reader**

PRAISE FOR CAROL BRUNEAU

These Good Hands

"A gripping novel with poetic insights into human behaviour and a rich sense of place."
–**Chronicle-Herald**

"A definite recommended read. I really came to connect, sympathize, and understand these characters. Camille in particular felt extraordinarily real. I connected with her passion and her desire to get more out of life. Bruneau has woven a powerful story that takes place alongside WWII, with characters who spring to life off of the page."
– **Worn Pages and Ink**

"Compassionate and richly textured, *These Good Hands* is one of those rare stories of female friendship that makes us grow in unsuspecting ways."
– **Eva Stachniak**, bestselling author of *The Winter Palace* and *Empress of the Night*

"[An] indelible novel of age, mental disorder and beauty."
– **The Sun Times**

Glass Voices

"This novel is so rich in detail and emotion that a first reading merely opens the reader to an appreciation of its gifts. Its density submerges the reader in a complete world of character, plot and setting.... *Glass Voices* illustrates the immense strength some people have to cope with tragedy—and that is truly inspiring."
–**The Globe and Mail**

"*Glass Voices* demonstrates how profoundly love shapes lives, no matter what else happens...textured and rich."
–**Quill & Quire**

"A remarkably intricate, textured and complex novel...deeply compassionate."
–**Literary Review of Canada**

Purple for Sky

"Carol Bruneau's *Purple for Sky*...will be this year's unheralded surprise. Bruneau has a saucy, punchy even ebullient writing style, and is completely at ease in the wonderful Arcadian milieu of the story."
–**The National Post**

"An endearing, entertaining tale by a first-class storyteller.... It is as meticulously crafted and multi-textured as the quilt that stands as the book's central metaphor."
–**The Globe and Mail**

"Reminiscent of Margaret Laurence's *The Stone Angel*....An intricate and compelling novel [that] holds a rich inventory of complex characters, historical details, and hard-won truths."
–**Atlantic Books Today**

Depth Rapture

"With her compassionate eye, her understanding of the human condition, her strong sense of place, her clean, lyrical prose, Carol Bruneau is an easy writer to praise. With her second collection of stories, she has shown herself to be one of the brightest lights in Atlantic fiction."
–**Pottersfield Portfolio**

"[I]t's the bold sense of bold-face confidence that makes these stories lethally strong and lethally true...an amazing progression for an astonishingly talented writer."
–**The Sunday Herald**

"The maturity and richness of a first-class storyteller."
–**The Globe and Mail**

a

BIRD

on

EVERY
TREE

Stories

CAROL
BRUNEAU

Vagrant
PRESS

Vagrant Press is an imprint of
Nimbus Publishing Limited
3731 Mackintosh St, Halifax, NS, B3K 5A5
(902) 455-4286 nimbus.ca

Printed and bound in Canada

NB1273
Cover image: *Frozen* by Lynn Misener, 2014, mixed media and oil

These stories are works of fiction. Names, characters, incidents, and places, including organizations and institutions, either are the product of the author's imagination or are used fictitiously.

The following stories were previously published: "The Race" in *Riddle Fence #20* (2015); "The Vagabond Lover" by Pottersfield Press in *Nova Scotia Love Stories* (2015); "Doves" by Goose Lane Editions in *Running the Whale's Back* (2013) and in *The Antigonish Review* (Spring 2005); "Polio Beach" by Breton Books in *Local Hero: New Cape Breton Stories* (2015).

Library and Archives Canada Cataloguing in Publication

Bruneau, Carol, 1956-
[Short stories. Selections]
A bird on every tree : stories / Carol Bruneau.
ISBN 978-1-77108-502-1 (softcover)
    I. Title.

PS8553 R854A6 2017   C813'.54   C2017-904095-2

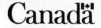  

Nimbus Publishing acknowledges the financial support for its publishing activities from the Government of Canada through the Canada Book Fund (CBF) and the Canada Council for the Arts, and from the Province of Nova Scotia. We are pleased to work in partnership with the Province of Nova Scotia to develop and promote our creative industries for the benefit of all Nova Scotians.

For the Spoonmaidens + one =
Cindy, Shawn, & DR

All nature seemed inclined to rest
But still there was no rest for me.
—"FAREWELL TO NOVA SCOTIA"

The time of the singing of birds is come,
and the voice of the turtle is heard in our land.
—SONG OF SOLOMON 2:10

Fish got to swim, birds got to fly.
—OSCAR HAMMERSTEIN II, *SHOWBOAT*

the RACE

THE ONLY THING I WAS EVER REALLY SCARED OF WAS DROWNING.
Being knocked out of the running—imagine—like being held back,
held under by some strange hand; and after all my practising, till I was
near blue! Dare anyone fault a girl for trying: so I told myself, knifing
through the chop, the Arm like a crumpled envelope. Nobody deserved
to win more than me, obvious even before the gun cracked, the sound
ringing over the cove.

A finer day would've helped, a fierce wind for July pushing against
us—all forty of us, gents and gals. One thing you could say for it: wind
didn't pick favourites, bloody offshore breeze whipping everything up,
rocking the gawkers in their dinghies—hundreds lining the route—
what you could see of them anyways, coming up for each breath. Boater
hats, cheering mouths. Mucky-mucks, mostly, a few I vaguely recognized but none that mattered. Fellas snapping photos, for the paper,
likely. The world-famous mixed long-distance race, they were touting it,

1

nearly half of us swimmers ladies, a few from as far away as Boston, here to show us slacker bluenosers what-for, I suppose. Three miles from the government wharf to the club with its swanky pool and boathouse, afternoon teas, tennis, and what-have-yous: the finish.

What, that little thing? All she has to do is look good. Sure I heard the comments, diving in. The water cold enough to turn your lungs to slob ice. Thrashing arms and legs all around and ahead of me, I let the snarky remarks sink away.

Arse in gear, Mar, eye on the prize. Delirium, maybe, but I could already see the picture framed: the silver trophy being hoisted into whose arms? Little Marion née McGinty's, that's whose. Notebook-juggling newsmen scribing away. Cameras flashing. In every shunt of seawater scalding my eyes, sure I could see it, the way I could hear them back in the old country—those who hadn't batted an eye seeing me go. Well, they'd have a different opinion when all around the globe the news flashed. *Not* that *Marion McGinty? Not ours?* Twenty-five-year-old beauty takes first prize in world's longest-ever mixed saltwater race. *Gad, is it ten years since she left us? That long?*

Winning wasn't a pipe dream. Not when you wanted something this fierce. Though the first quarter-mile not behind me, I could feel the numbing while I pushed back that crazy fear, keeping afloat of it.

The last person that one can afford to let down is herself.

So the water became turf, my hands trowels but for the pins and needles. Legs, scissors; arms and shoulders, fly wheels, till pretty much my whole body was no longer a letter-knife but a sewing machine stitching a straight seam through whitecaps. Snip-snip, stitch-stitch. A weave of muscle crawling through spray, I heaved and hewed my way. *Always knew what she wanted, Marion did, whether it suited anyone else or not.* Well, the one thing I wasn't was a quitter. *No quitter ever profits,* slosh-glugged in both ears. The Arm pure crystal cleaving all around—a thousand chandeliers smashing, it could've been—and a spotter in a dinghy yelling through a bullhorn: The half-mile mark!

Chandeliers like my husband Willard had promised would light every room—what a load, that. As good as the rocks so many fathoms below. Who had to see to know they lurked? Dumb as clouds under the crashing surface, they'd have thrown me off had I been fool enough to glance down.

The one time I *had* looked down, crossing this very stretch of water, gad, the sight near docked me from where I'd been headed. The one time I'd been colder than now—all but my feet, that is—when I could've, should've taken those rocks as a sign, a sign of what lay ahead. But who isn't an ignoramus at fifteen, and if in this world you expect a snowball's chance in hell of succeeding, best not to bellyache. So I told the thunder in my head, its frozen, stinging burble in my nose and ears and the back of my throat. Because the worst could've happened that time but didn't. Jesus, Mary, Joseph, and all the saints must've been with me. Because I'd made it then, hadn't I?

Mind on the race, Mar. Mind on the race.

One mile!

One and a quarter miles!

Yet the aching cold brought it back: the wintry day I landed in this godforsaken place, by sea naturally; the rocks under ice. Who knew then salt water froze into a road? No one to meet me at the docks, sweep me off my feet, slather me with kisses—not even Willard's poker-faced relations. But a man who stamped my papers gave directions, another carted my bag partway, for free—no skin off my neck, a little flirting into the bargain, flashing my wedding band. My hair a snarl from the week-long crossing. Some took me for being a touch older than I was, on account of it perhaps?

One and a half miles!

Fastest way to get there is on foot, darlin'. Over the Arm, I was told, a branch of the harbour so great it didn't freeze. My husband of two weeks a thousand million miles away—on a boat to France or in a foxhole? We'd met in London. I'd just arrived from Belfast. Marry me, he'd said, his offer not unappealing. A different life, a better life, one that involved automobiles and not walking wherever you went. Dining off fine china in a house with so many rooms you could get lost. His family's digs a thousand times grander than anything you'd find here, he said. An estate overlooking the sea, with a view of ships coming and going, and the best neighbours around, treating you as their own. Leave the fighting to Europe—Yurp, he called it—and the peace and quiet to them back home. What wasn't to like over there on the better side of the ocean?

One and three-quarter miles! Then two! Two, and one left to go! Three in the lead, well past the midway mark! a voice blasted from the bullhorn, all but drummed out by the tumbling water. The rip and ride of muscle, shoulder blades, hips, knees, ankles—it was like I could no longer feel any of these parts, only hear their workings, and my salt-blinded eyes fixed on nothing, all of me unmoored as a buoy bobbing off, to be caught between the rocks and gliding keels?

Marion, Marion: you're losing ground, girl! Eye on the prize, eye on the prize: focus! But all my buoy-eyes took in were jets, eruptions, spurts, and flashes—a glimpse of animals sounding ahead, far ahead. Swimmers like seals. The burn in my back either a gaff hook or an anchor.

That long-lost winter evening the rocks might well have been clouds in a night sky. Watch me walk on water! I fended off the old voices nattering about 'thin places.' The howling cold, the suppertime dusk streaked with red, nothing in my belly since the ship's sad lunch. 'Sweetpea,' the baggage handler had called me, directing me around the tip of a wooded point to a wharf embedded in ice, a path shovelled in the snow. Smarter, I'd have pocketed Willard's ring, to be pawned later on, all my earthly goods in that sole bag. *Lucky thing you were born pretty, Mar. Looks are about all you've got.* And lucky thing snow marked both sides of that straight black strip over the ice. The wind fit to blow me past the edge, where a seal lolled—a great slug of a beast but not as threatening as whatever creatures lurked on land, nothing but thick dark forest stretching up from either shore. Sprinklings of light here and there, from the tiniest of hovels huddled below a bluff. The wind enough to wring tears. The soles of my boots skidding along, my bag a deadweight and certain to shame me when I reached Willard's parents'.

You'll have the finest glad rags cash can buy, Marion McGinty: another of his promises. Granted, I knew my husband little more than in the biblical way when we parted. His arms made a cosy belt around my waist, his height a mantle draped over me. Tall, he was, but no giant, and in no way remarkable other than for the gift of gab and one other talent, drawing. Cartoons sketched on wallpaper lifted from where we roomed, between our meeting and my departure. He promised me the northern stars while drawing the Kaiser and a pack of bayonet-wielding troops. Marching, they were, always marching—something invisible putting the boots to them. The way it put the boots to me crossing the ice, and now, immersed in the drink, the sea.

4

It was pitch dark that day when I reached shore, or the shore reached me. Lookin' for the Lesters? they said, the first place I tried. Up thataway, see? Past the school and the dip in the road, can't miss it if you don't blink. Picturing Willard, I wondered what he was eating, where he was sleeping. Something better than nothing and someplace warmer than here, I'd felt sinkingly sure.

The burning stopped. The cold stopped. The churning fountain ahead of me veered off. At the edge of my bobbing sight pink skin flashed, well, bluish-pink, purple. A girl was being hauled into a boat by an octopus—a mess of arms. That's all there was time to see. Warm arms, warming flesh. The salt tasted like blood, or was blood become salt? I was no longer warm- but cold-blooded; no longer had lungs, but gills. I'd drowned, sure, just didn't know it yet.

If you quit, you'll have a snowball's chance of thawing, being warm again.

It might've been sea smoke, not spray, clouding my sight. The ocean boiling on a frigid February night, offering its vapour to the heavens. But sense pulled me back. You can still win this, Mar. Another boat rode alongside, close, too close—get out of my way! More octopus arms, a fountain's jets silenced: another opponent plucked out of the running. Plucked upwards, lifted—a mockery, a trick to make quitting look easy, sensible? My brain cramped around the thought.

Voices were shouting. Less than three-quarters of a mile to go! We were neck and neck—first the shiny blue of a bathing cap, then the seal-black of another head. This one lagged, lagged, floated, taunting me, mocking me, sure: a bluish log adrift, rolling onto its back, then being retrieved from the chop. Sure, I'd drowned. Sure, my gills had stopped working. In a spasm I'd downed an ocean's worth of water? Eye on the prize. Don't let yourself be sidetracked, hoodwinked, do *not*. But the old voices were a chilly clamour: *Marion McGinty, who do you think you are?*

Marion Lester to you, was how I'd introduced myself. The woman who answered the door having no clue who or what I might be. Finally letting me in, she wept to hear of Willard. So it's good news, not bad? He's well? My boy is well! Not a moment's regard for the daughter-in-law who'd sailed so far, then crossed the ice. Grudgingly, she put soup on the table, told me to sit. Starving, I had little appetite for her greasy broth. Who knew a flat in Belfast stuffed with thirteen people, my parents, brothers, and sisters, could be more than matched by this place of promises? There, at least, would have been hugs and a fireside bed. But Willard's mother provided a curtained-off cot upstairs, herself and three grown men snoring nearby. The water in the wash basin froze so I took my hairbrush to it—the silver-handled one my husband bought as a wedding gift to match the mirror he said mimicked the shape of my face.

But he's already got a girl, you know, here in the Cove.

In the Cove, in the Arm, appendages of the bigger, broader harbour and the sea stretching clear to Europe—what is she, a mermaid? I said. Staying on, I determined to write to him, describing my complaint. And the ice melted, eventually, so that it was no longer possible to cross the water on foot, but only by open boat. Which was how I made excursions to town—and got around, I don't mind saying—when I wasn't watching ships passing in the channel beyond, from the porch of his family's home with its mud cellar and outhouse, and a small, stony brook running past, emptying into the cove. At night I listened to it, the only music to drown out the sounds of his parents and brothers sleeping. As the nature of my complaint grew so might their affections, I thought; they would have to.

Willard will make a fine dad, another reason for the war to end and for him to come home, said my mother-in-law, Margaret. She happily put me to work. Since you're here you'd best make yourself useful. Impossible to go about unnoticed, watched like some foreigner come to pinch the cutlery. If there'd been any worth pinching.

He was shorter than I remembered, and thinner, when his ship finally came in; his shock of dark hair dulled and greasy, eyes the same; and he startled at the sound of pennies dropping into the pantry tin. His mother's cache, splurged on butter and milk because her boy had returned from the war. At night he turned his eyes away, clinging to me like a piece of cork. If only I could've drifted off. It was like treading over shell ice while waiting for a thaw, for something, anything to shift and take me away. That fall I gave birth to a girl he named after his mother—in thanks for her looking after me.

Of course Margaret's your daughter, I said; do the arithmetic, you've got the fingers.

I didn't raise you. But you're all right, Margaret One said to me, just the once. Like squeezing juice from a plum pit. A small version of her granny was Margaret Two, who, in her child's way, thrived. There was talk of Willard going to the United States, to New York, Chicago, even Hollywood, California, to make a living at drawing cartoons. Right, and I've got a cellar full of whale blubber I'll sell you cheap, his mother said; and for once she and I were agreed.

I doubt he'd have taken Margaret, our daughter, with him.

At night, crammed between them in the cot, I'd dream, a strange dream in which I was a gull perched on the bluff, granted a view not just of the cove but the rubble on its bottom. The skeletons of boats, broken bottles—no treasure, mind—even a piano, with barnacled keys. The remains of a horse and a good-sized cart, and dogs, the dreadful frozen carcasses of dogs. Luckily I'd wake before seeing human ones, the scattered bodies of any who'd gone through the ice, eyes eaten away by creatures creeping over the seabed, well beyond the rocks. I would wake, and so much for sleeping in: Margaret One brimming with plans for me, scrubbing, cooking, and, any spare moments, keeping Margaret Two out of her hair. Willard too:

Every kid should know how to swim. Whyn't you teach her?

Teach her yourself. You're her da.

But I found myself one stifling July day leading the child up the rocky path to the pond in the woods. Like a bowl of boiled tea dark as your arse, rushes all around it, and wild laurel and huckleberry bushes, and bullfrogs snapping their jaws or limbs, however they made their noise. Sure I'd been a swimmer in Belfast; dare me to dive in anywhere and out-swim anyone. But it was salt water I liked, not brown murk. And didn't Margaret Two toddle off a rock and down, down—just the top of her reddish curls floating up like a jellyfish before disappearing altogether.

Don't just frigging stand there! What are ya, froze? Are ya that stunned a mother?

Wasn't it Flossie Brunt, the gal Willard had been sweet on, who jumped in, clothes and all, and saved her—my little girl's face fish-white as I fussed and fretted over her, and slowly, slowly got her breathing again. I confess, it was like some dreadful thing had wrapped itself round my ankles and chained me there.

CAROL BRUNEAU

Some mother you are. If I hadn't of been there, what, you'd of let her drown? Scared of getting your feet wet?

You little bitch, said Margaret One when it got around.

It could've happened to anyone, Willard said.

The dreams worsened. I'd see Margaret Two in her little smocked dress, a bow in her hair, lying on the bottom like a doll. Except her face was her grandmother's, and I'd see myself resting beside her, peepers wide open, deader than dead. No Willard, though. No longer nervous as a cat, in the dream he was enjoying the high life in the USA, sitting under a palm tree at a drawing table, drinking whisky on ice and sketching his heart out, Margaret One waiting on him hand and foot.

To be fair, the old woman wasn't all bad. The only way to get over your fears is facing 'em, she told Willard, staring him down when the clang of a pot lid would send him under the table. A grown man! Giving me the evil eye, she'd go back to spoiling Margaret Two, stuffing her with molasses kisses. Bribes, if you ask me, as I tried not to think they were two peas in a pod, a pebble—Willard—between them.

By the time the girl was seven, I swear she had the old doll's scowl.

How'd a looker like you spawn her? that hateful Flossie Brunt had the gall to say, once.

Yeah? I'll show you who you're talking at.

Watched your own kid near-drownded. You've showed me all right.

Who knows what her beef was? Common knowledge by now what a basket case poor Willard was.

Jealous, are you?

Not that it mattered; by then I'd been rescued, more or less. But when word of the upcoming race ran in the paper, I had an idea what she was up to, Flossie the 'best swimmer this end of the cove.' Skinny legs on her, wouldn't last five minutes out there, spending all summer performing her strokes in Tea Lake; I happened to know for a fact, perfecting mine offshore. Sure, she'd chicken out even before the gun went off.

As it happened, she didn't. But as I hacked and sliced up to the two-and-a-half-mile mark, I had no care or thought of Flossie Brunt or anybody, except the man I knew in town. A benefactor, you could say. The one who'd found me a position in the office of his friend, an ophthalmologist's, as a matter of fact. A dogged word, that, whose rhythm

8

matched my strokes: one two three four five, *breathe*. Even though I could no longer see or hear a bleeding thing—neither cheering onlookers nor splashes and bobs ahead—all I knew was I mustn't look back. Somewhere behind me, sure, Flossie Brunt would be mussel-blue, the air shivering with her curses. Flossie not the only one colder than a brass monkey's balls in February.

The man in my mind, the one who'd entered me in the competition, had a warm, soft heart, a wife, and two sweet daughters to prove it. All I had to do, in exchange for a splendid little flat—an entire floor to myself, leaded glass in the entry—was entertain him now and then. So I'd already won, when you look at it that way; the race another thing altogether—icing on the cake, sure, if I pulled it off. If I lived to pull it off. Not that things were ever simple or straightforward. Not after what I'd been through. Not after the effort required. A solid string of burn lifting my head up, then lowering it, up then down, and my arms too: I was a puppet to the waves. Besides that string, I could barely feel anything now.

Well, Mar, you always did find your way, a voice very like my mother's seemed to call out. If you've got hopes for yourself other than cleaning some rich lady's house and wiping her brats' arses, you'd best have a plan. One's as good as another. Choose me, Willard had said; my benefactor too, my face doing all the talking necessary. Snooze and you lose; you're dead a long time. That's what old Margaret, my mother-in-law, would say; not that I'd needed her permission to walk away from there. And just as I took a briny lungful, a commotion stirred: some poor gangly thing—a cadaver?—being lifted up and away; or maybe I was dreaming it? Maybe, since I could no longer feel where my body ended and my tarry soul began, it was me? Drowned dead in the final heat, dragged up and away, a loser.

Except in my ears the glug became a hiss, like every flat in every corner of the city had its taps turned on, running—a hiss that whistled and shuddered and pushed deeper than water or air ever could. A hiss that was sharper and deeper and louder than any fish or engines or oars could make, louder than the blood thumping my ears; and through it bloomed faces, gunwales, hands, hands reaching and waving—and my knees struck rock, pebbles, the squish of mud, the rippling glimmer of upside-down trees breaking around me.

Trees, grass, and the white-and-green of the boathouse, these I saw, and the flare of sunlight not flashbulbs. I saw myself all alone, in those seconds before arms boosted me up and onto shore. Not another swimmer to be seen, and in my confusion—the blinding sunlight painting everything with blackness—I knew I'd come in last. If hell has a tint to it, sure it must be green like the lapping water as I was lifted—or maybe it was purgatory. I confess it was Willard's face that bobbed in my head as they plunked me on a platform, at the foot of the terraced lawn. Will you not even think about coming back to us? he was saying in my head, as they bundled towels round me and raised my dead stick-arms skyward. But they were screaming out my name—not the old voices but real ones.

I only knew they were real when they pricked me pinning the ribbon to my chest. And a fellow with a notebook stuck his face into mine: So, Miss Marion Lester. Came up outta nowhere, now you're the champ. How does it feel?

The life coming back into me. "Words can't begin—," I said.

DOVES

IT IS A LONG WAY FROM LAGOS TO GREYSTONE, AND GOD'S WILL that brings me here. His hand steers the car into the frozen, bumpy parking lot. Helping Hand, says the sign. Put your hand in the hand: music stirs in my head, clapping too. The sound of clapping hands, marching feet; of people on the move, dancing in the Spirit. But on this most bitter of days, Mission Monday, there is no time for singing. There is work to be done.

The woman inside greets me, smiles as if seeing the Holy Mother. I swing my bag up onto the counter, mittens collected by the diocese.

"Any large ones?" She mouths the words wide as if that will aid my understanding. My face is so cold I do not speak, emptying out the contents. A mother with a small boy comes up and rummages.

"You givin' these away? Or do we gotta buy 'em?" The mother looks past me, past my hands, which are starting to thaw. She has a blue rucksack tucked under her arm. The boy clutches an orange plastic gun.

There are rules regarding such donations, rules too often broken. His eyes are milky brown, like a river. There is mud—chocolate—around his mouth. He grabs a mitten; his mother slaps his hand.

"Don't touch, I said. How many times I gotta tell you?" The mother's voice is a nail splitting wood—she jerks the boy's arm—"Wha'd I say?" and the boy drops the mitts in the puddle at our feet.

My veil sweeps my cheek as I retrieve them. Wiping them off, I hold them out. The boy slaps them away, and the mother swats his head. I retrieve them again and pass them to her. But her eyes move past me and fix on the woman behind the counter, who blinks and says, "Take them."

We see so many mothers like this, Sister Marcetta and I: pale white girls pushing strollers, with their thin white boyfriends wearing ball caps. They choose clothes that don't look warm enough and they smoke, looking at us in a way that makes me want to cover my face. The look is cold and shameless. God forgive me for throwing stones. It is the children in the strollers whom Jesus gathers to Himself; for whom Marcetta and I most gratefully labour.

"The peace of the Lord be with you," I say softly. The boy aims his weapon, lets it fall to his side.

"Put that down, I toldja. I'm not buyin' nothing."

Clothing is free to those who cannot pay, though the sale of donations funds our work. I pray for patience and to not grow weary, and that the love of Jesus will spill from my heart into the hearts of others.

The woman behind the counter says, "Sister, if you wouldn't mind—"

There is sorting to be done, and I am in charge of it. Pots and pans, children's books, baby clothes, and women's dresses such as Jezebel, wife of Ahab, might wear. Everything comes in large green garbage bags stuffed to overflowing. The donations are so plentiful they could be things collected after a famine perhaps, or a massacre—but they are clean, of course, if threadbare. Today there is a girl to help me, a volunteer named Tina.

"Tina," I say. "What is that short for?"

"Christina," she says, not looking up. The thing most noticeable in this mission is how the helpers and the helped look past you, as if talking to a bystander. As if they see your guardian angel, and it is she, not you, who is speaking.

"What should I do with this?" Tina asks. It looks like a man's belt, studded dangerously with chrome. "My boyfriend wants one just like it," she hints, and smiles, and tucks it inside her coat. She isn't dressed for the cold either, the skin above her slacks so very white, white as milk watered down to nourish a multitude.

"Sister Berthe?" The girl's voice is flat, and I think of the doulas whom Sister Marcetta enlists to attend mothers giving birth to babies without fathers. I can't help but look at this girl's stomach; the way she has no stomach at all but doesn't look hungry. No one here looks hungry for anything but guidance. The light of Christ, who came into the world so that we might see.

"Yes, my child," I say, a pair of trousers folded over my arm and many pairs more to sort and hang.

"Shit—oh, shoot. Someone needs help."

The woman from behind the counter appears. Her grin confuses me; her eyes are hard and grey as the roadway. Before I can step from the sorting area into the display room full of clothing, broken toys, mugs, plates, ashtrays, and plastic flowers, there's a shout, a cry that sends needles up my spine. Buses and cars spit, shooting past just outside.

"What is it, my child?"

The man before me has wild hair, as though he has stood for days on a mountain in the freezing wind. His eyes spin and dart. He's wearing a torn quilted coat, gold in colour, gold as threshed wheat. His hands are bare and chapped and he wrings them—to warm them, perhaps. But then he waves them, his hands a burning bush of activity, a firestorm, and he curtsies the way people curtsy for Queen Elizabeth, a trip-step then up again, and pushes himself past my outstretched arms. Briefly I feel his breath on my face and catch his smell; it is the smell of spiritual hunger: too much wine at the wedding feast.

Tina and the woman from the counter shy behind a rack of coats— worn, thick woollen coats that make me think of sheep, of sacrifices made to God before our washing in the Blood of the Lamb. The woman, whose name escapes me, clears her throat and gasps. As if spotting a body swinging past in a current. Parting the sea of rags, I peer through. The man with wild eyes is urinating on the furniture, a plaid sofa that would have gone free to whomever asked. Seek and ye shall find; ask and it shall be given.

"Get out. Get out now," the woman orders. "You are not welcome in this place." Her voice is stony as the soil of our mission, and as cold as the dawn when, on Fridays, I rise to prepare the small white wafers for Holy Communion. Just in case, as Sister Marcetta says.

The man zips his pants, wipes his nose. His gaze is cast downwards. There is a roll of Lifesaver candies beside the cash box, and I peel one away and offer it. He puts his tongue out as if to receive the Host. It calms him and, thank the Lord, the community of saints, and all the archangels, he turns, shrugging his shoulders, and leaves.

When all the garbage bags have been emptied and their contents sorted, I take the volunteers' hands and we pray in a small circle. Their hands are pale as fish, and I think of the miracle of the loaves and fishes, the feeding of the five thousand. Such a numbering of the hungry challenges me: I see multitudes of the living coursing down dusty streets. I see rivers running red.

"See ya next week," Tina shouts, following me to the car, carrying the large white mittens I have almost forgotten. Sister Marcetta was kind enough to provide them, along with a gift of lock de-icer. It's a very long way from Lagos, Satan's voice cajoles as I scrape frost from the car.

"God be with you," I call out. "Bless you, dear. Bless you."

At the convent, Sister Marcetta mashes potatoes for the hungry who will partake of the Hot Meal held near the mall. I think of the man in the quilted coat, and of mothers and dark-skinned babies, and pray silently for new ways to serve the Lord. Marcetta mixes in an egg, margarine, and bluish milk for extra nutrition, and sets aside a dishful for us. Putting on boots she calls mukluks, she carries the pot to her car. Just the tip of the cross in our front yard shows above the snow; it's as plain as a grave marker when there aren't the means for something permanent. The blue security sign is buried, too. I vaguely recall the presence of grass.

"Don't forget the wash," Sister calls. "Man the fort. Good luck!"

Waving, I think of the Juju market where people purchase wares for voodoo: shrivelled heads of animals, paws and teeth. You're not to think of luck, we counsel the sorrowful, who appear at odd hours seeking our prayers. It has nothing to do with luck: it is grace, we tell them. God's will, I remind myself, reeling our habits from the line. Dancing stiffly in the bitter gusts, they resemble pieces of sky, their cotton the same lavender blue of forget-me-nots, Sister says. To me it is the Virgin's blue: the blue of sorrows, abandonment.

This is my afternoon for contemplation, but first there are chores: mending, the basement pews to be polished. With its red candle burning day and night like the Sacred Heart, our chapel is Golgotha, a place of bones bleached white as this landscape. But we have no Stations of the Cross, nor do we have a regular priest, which grieves us when the faithful come to say confession. *You are marching in the light of Christ*, an inner voice promised when I departed Nigeria. With gunshots echoing through the heat, I was glad to board the plane. But the rosy light of the sanctuary brings back the sound of soldiers, and I trudge upstairs.

Sister Marcetta has collected the clothing from the supermarket bin, a mountain of it serviceable with repair. I contemplate her machine in the kitchen, on which she plays her CDs, inspirational ones like *Eternal Light: Music of Inner Peace*, my favourite. But it's all too easy to get lost in it, and one must be ready, always ready, not just for the faithful, but for all seeking respite from woe. Since the priest stopped coming, Sister and I have been forced to break rules, our duty being to listen and lighten burdens.

"I'm addicted, Sister," a woman confessed once, "to that stuff on the internet." Her hands flapped like helpless doves. "Every Wednesday Satan tells me to play the slots. He's there, Sister. Honest to God, right there in my bathroom, under the sink." What does one say? Go forth, my child; gamble your life away? It is meet and right to take chances?

The bell rings as I thread the needle, a small pair of trousers over my knee. The sound jars the stillness. I descend the stairs. The caller's shape looms through the entry's pebbled glass. Blurred, he appears agitated, his hair a bush in a fierce gale. Hesitating but a moment, I quickly open the door, hear a gasp—my own. I recognize his coat; it is gold and puffy, with stains on the front.

"How may we be of service, brother?" It takes extra breath to push this out.

He holds a shoebox in his gloveless hands. My eyes flit to the label: Airwalk.

The man snarls like a wild dog. Before I can speak again, he lifts the lid. What I see surprises me, shocks me a little but not very much. Not when you have seen the dead in rivers and roadways. It is a pigeon, its feathers layered grey like billowing smoke. There's a greenish-pink shine around its staring eye. Its wing sticks up like that of a chicken about to be roasted.

"Service," the man mutters. "Please ma'am. Help me. I have to bury him."

It takes me a moment to comprehend. He tugs at my sleeve, tugs so sharply I fear it will rip. I explain, rather quickly, that the priest no longer makes regular calls, the need being insufficiently great.

"All things bright and beauteeeful," the man says. "Don't you think he deserves a decent burial?"

But I am thinking of the priest's final visit, to hear the confessions of a grandmother and her daughter. The faithful are seldom men; of course, it was women who found Jesus risen from the tomb. Women like the gambling lady who came to me, asking, "Life is about taking risks am I right, Sister? God spoke to me in a dream," she said. "There's this man, see? He's gonna meet me in Kissimmee."

"What is this Kissimmee?"

"Sister, you don't want to know: it's warm there."

"You must listen to what your heart tells you."

"Like, I met this guy on the 'net."

"Listen to the Spirit. He's there to guide you."

"Now Sister, the heart and the Spirit, ain't they the same?"

After a time their faces—those of the faithful and the afflicted—are faces in a river.

The man replaces the lid and shakes the box. Its contents thud against cardboard. "Sister!" His voice relocates me, the look in his eyes angry, indignant. He clutches the shoebox to his chest. I think rather idly of the security system—the sign on its post beneath the snow. A buzzer meant to deter intruders will sound unless you disable it. The buzzer makes Marcetta nervous. Once it went off accidentally, the police came, and the convent was billed—an amount that could have provided food for many. His will be done on earth as it is in heaven.

The man gazes at the front of my habit. Someone—the gambler making her confession—called us bluebirds, Marcetta and me. She seemed a decent person, put five dollars in the donations box on her way out to her car. She has not returned, and I wonder how things are in Kissimmee, whether she and the internet man have tied the knot, been blessed in Holy Matrimony.

My brother with the pigeon slackens; his shoulders droop. I no longer see the man who spoiled the sofa, and whom the volunteer cast out. He isn't much more than a boy, really. Below his wild hair his face is flat, white, swollen, with a spray of pimples on his jaw. His mouth resembles a fish's. "Help me, Miss," he begs. The look in his eyes is one I have seen before, in the eyes of men running with knives through the streets.

"You got a church here," he says, and his gaze climbs the small flight of stairs to the kitchen, to the clean white curtains, the sink, the table, walls spotless and bare but for a crucifix. Cold, cold air blows in past him, filling the stairwell.

"There's no priest, I'm sorry. No one to conduct a funeral, I'm afraid." I keep my voice gentle, imagining Sister Marcetta at the soup kitchen, her nervousness if she returned now. *You are not welcome in this building*, she too has told undesirables.

"We must open our hearts to the stranger," I've reminded her, but Marcetta can be set in her ways.

The man-boy begins to weep, a gruff coughing.

"Come with me," I say softly. "Are you hungry?" Sister Marcetta would not approve, but I lead him to the kitchen, take a sandwich from the refrigerator. The bread is very white; everything about this place is so. He looks like he is eating snow, devouring it—a jackal that has not eaten in some time. The food soothes him. The dominion of God is suddenly vast and in the man's calm I am a refugee, nation-less before God's will. My life exists without borders. Sometimes it seems I will never comprehend the ways of this frozen place, but as Marcetta says, it is up to us to cast the seeds. Only the Lord can make them grow.

I boil water, stir the powdered coffee in. His dirty hands reach for the cup.

"Will you take care of it for me, Sister?" he says meekly, and I remember the box on the stairs. "Can you gimme a lift somewheres, Sister?"

I think of my car, how it will need to be scraped again, and Sister Marcetta's instructions as she loaded the pot into hers.

"Sister. I need a drive to my girlfriend's." Once more the man looks around like a hungry animal.

· Allow me, Lord, to open my heart, to open my life to you. The stranger.

"I know you got the keys to your car here someplace," he says.

I take them from the hook beneath the cupboard, and put on my coat. He ignores the shoebox by the mat. "Leave it," he says, when I go to pick it up.

The car does not want to start at first. "Don't flood it," he says, and I think of the river full of rags. His breathing makes an ocean sound in my ears. "I shore appreciate this."

My hands on the wheel tremble, not from the engine's vibration so much as the pulse of fear, as he directs me through a zigzag of streets. Oh Holy Spirit, Counsellor: what wilderness have you led me into?

Outside a small house he orders me to stop. The tires skid on the icy road and my chest contracts. Holding my breath, I pray for the guidance of the Counsellor, the blameless, ever-present Comforter.

"Wait here." His coat rides up as he gets out. The motor tick-tick-ticks as he slouches to the door and lets himself in. I think of Marcetta finding the shoebox but no sign of me.

"Cherished and Holy Infant," I pray aloud.

The man reappears with a paper bag under his arm and gets in, telling me to drive again. I hear the slosh as he uncaps the bottle inside and drinks, a long slurp, as I try to keep my gaze on the road.

The Spirit led the Saviour into the wilderness, not *in* the wilderness. Thou shalt worship the Lord thy God, He said, and Him only shalt thou serve. I want to cross myself but my hand won't leave the wheel.

"Got some thirst, boy," the man apologizes. "Just a little errand, Sister." But his voice grows sharp again. "Right here. Left there. Right, now! At these lights," he directs. "Now drive. That's right. Now. See them lights?"

Deliver me, Lord.

Obeying, I turn onto a road that climbs a hill higher than the one on which our convent sits. Children slog over the snowbanks. A few look slightly familiar; perhaps they have visited the Helping Hand. We pass rows and rows of buildings, their homes perhaps. Many have boarded-up windows.

Thou shalt not tempt the Lord thy God.

"A ghost town," I observe, my voice quaking, and he smirks.

"Shut up!"

Quietly I pray, "Our Father, who art—"

"Shut up with that God stuff!" He pushes the bottle at me, its neck nudging my coat.

Oh Lord, forgive me all my transgressions.

Up and up the hill we drive, miles and miles it seems, past more of these houses. Some have Christmas ornaments flapping in the wind. Big sheets of foil in the windows, big metal doors, barricades. I think of the faithful and all their confessions, of the woman in Kissimmee.

"Welcome to Greystone, Sister." He laughs.

"When"—I swallow—"did your bird die, sir?"

He scowls, and the liquor slides back down the neck of the bottle. "Bird?" he says, and barks something unrepeatable. Before us the top of the hill shines, the snow's brilliance reflecting the afternoon sun. In front of the last row of houses the man shouts, "Right here, Sister. This is where my girlfriend lives. You better wait, though, till I see if she's home."

The tires bite into ice. I'm perspiring. In the name of the Father, and of the Son...against my heart's advice I park. The heater has finally come on, emitting a dry burst of heat. Perspiration twists under my clothing, a clammy wetness. Still I am grateful for the heater and for my heavy coat, and give thanks—for it and for Sister Marcetta and even her catalogue, the one she brought to me before the snow arrived, filled with every imaginable good. Choose a good warm coat and boots, she said and placed the order; such was her welcome.

In the name of—I imagine her juggling the empty pot, wrestling it and the shoebox upstairs.

A child answers the door and the man pushes inside. Through the strips of tinsel in the window he waves to me, like a priest passing benediction. Lord have mercy.

Tears of gratitude blur my vision. Wiping my eyes, I bow my head and breathe. Next door someone appears with a large black dog on a chain. Neither looks as I pull away. By now Sister will be warming our supper, dividing the bowl of potato, mixing it with leftover meat.

My stomach races with hunger; this climate feeds the body's appetite where heat would stifle it. The sun is a low orange glare shining off every surface now, and carefully I proceed downhill, wondering about the man's girlfriend and the child—his child? Perhaps I should have stopped, knocked, made sure the child was all right, that there was food. Something other than the brown paper bag under his arm.

The same children are still climbing the snowbanks uphill. They look like small, bright-coated animals squirming towards me.

Please, Lord Jesus, forgive my selfishness and sins of omission.

A car comes racing up behind, passing, its tires making a hissing sound.

I see the boy, the one from this morning, from the Helping Hand, the one with the plastic gun. He is walking the top of the snowbank like an astronaut exploring the moon. His face is wide and pale, so pale, like all the faces in our mission. Even his hair is pale as he turns and shouts to his friends. He has the blue rucksack strapped to his back, and takes big floppy steps in his boots.

As the snow breaks and spills, he slips and the car before me skids and spins.

The thud is like the Lord's fist coming down. All I see are the boots flying up, one a little higher than the other, then falling like heavy, flapping birds.

I don't even feel the slip of the seat belt as I jump out. The rusty blue car sits across the road. Its driver takes a long moment to appear. A white man with a dirty growth of beard and a ball cap, he could be the boyfriend of any of the mothers we minister to, Sister Marcetta and I. Perhaps he is coming home from the supper Marcetta has helped serve.

He sucks a cigarette, sucks it as if it were a mother's nipple, as the two of us kneel over the boy.

My heart turns hollow, my soul like the hot-cold roar inside a seashell plucked from the scorching sand of a beach.

Children, rosy-cheeked and smelling of school and damp clothing, press around us, the driver and me, and the boy who lies limp and cold on the icy pavement.

Only my soul hears. An anguished noise, hysteria. If there are words, voices, they float far above us, like a hurricane wind threshing the palms.

Already the boy's face is turning grey as the slush. A sliver of orange plastic sticks out from his jacket, but there is no blood. His eyes are closed. His mouth is serene, peaceful, without a hint of astonishment or surprise. I put my hand over his heart. Someone folds a scarf, places it under his head.

Tenderly, trembling with the love of Jesus in my throat, I make the sign of the cross.

The driver waits in his car, the engine running. Glancing back, I believe I see the pigeon man's face in the window, but he does not come outside. I take off my coat and cover the boy with it. It covers him from head to toe, his body is so small. It surprises me, how small.

The air freezes my breath. I don't want to leave the boy; I will not leave him. The wind pulls and tugs at my habit. It is a cold that scorches, but I no longer feel it. The sting is in the wait for the authorities—the ambulance and the police—who eventually arrive and take our statements.

I do not even know the boy's name. His mother is merely a voice scratching in my head, a pair of hands holding mittens.

"Sister Berthe Uledi Adumi," I offer my identity, "Order of the Eucharistic Heart." No one blinks, or bats an eye. It was an accident: God knows this, I tell the authorities and everyone who will listen. No one contests my statement. The driver, whose name becomes a single sound, smokes and kicks the snow, smokes and scratches beneath his cap, keeping his lips drawn tight.

It is dusk when we are free to go, the orange sky aflame and the street lights blazing as I drive slowly through the blackened streets. The traffic lights remind me of Lifesaver candies and the colours of Kwanzaa. In this wilderness everything is black now, red and yellow and green.

At the convent Sister Marcetta has placed the shoebox under the back step, and taken up the mending that I have neglected.

She lays her hands on me as we kneel before each other to pray. It is a special prayer, which we offer before the tiny altar, with the light of Christ's sacred gift burning brightly. The kingdom of heaven is like the tiniest seed, a mustard seed, He said, which grows into the largest of bushes for the birds of the air to come and lodge in its branches.

Through my tears I promise to do one thing: I will bury this bird in the back yard, as soon as the ground thaws enough to work. With this promise made, we pray deep into the night for the rocks and the trees, the grass and the soil; for the good of all children, the seeds of our mission, whether or not they take root.

BLUE SHADOWS

THE DAY BEGAN WITH GREENHOUSES, KREMLIN-ESQUE DOMES OF icy glass, the glitter of sunlight through vapour—or costume jewelry set in the snow. That's what they resembled, rhinestones in the middle of a park ringed by the down-and-out congregating on benches. Passing these people always felt like an issue, the promise of steamy warmth and silence drawing me forward—the breath of plants—my baby asleep against me in her carrier. You know what it's like, holding a newborn bundled against winter. Such compact warmth, a miraculous heater against your chest.

That baby smell, the powdery skin, the rip of razor-sharp little fingernails contained by mittens. I'd just clipped Anna's with my teeth before setting out. The thought of bringing anything remotely metal near those tiny fingertips enough to make me quiver, my inner parts slowly knitting back together after giving birth—the shock of it, and the bearish feeling, that you could claw someone's eyes out to prevent their harming the baby: my baby.

So, this morning. Sleep-deprived, addled, and needing warmth I sought company, only the kind that didn't talk. Just to know that life breathed beyond Anna and me, and her dad of course. The moistness of her angora scarf against her mouth, her pink tuque squeezed down over her eyes—rosy cheeks, tiny nose showing, three miniscule white dots there: infant acne. The perfect weight of a helpless child was my shield as I moved past the benches, past outstretched hands, gloveless, burled with cold and bloodied knuckles. "Spare change, miss? I need a cuppa coffee, miss." My worst fear that one of those hands would touch Anna.

Morning was always trickiest—the nearby shelter emptying till nightfall—but the best time to visit this place. The greenhouses were open year round. But the winter light and the loneliness of new motherhood made them attractive now, though riding the streetcar the long months of pregnancy I'd barely noticed them. Mat leave felt like retirement from my media job, the job I'd left Halifax for, the one that had led to my meeting Tom. This time off was a strange hiatus, a soporific suspension—a guilty pleasure somehow, though I'd done nothing wrong. Unless you're one of those types who fault people for bringing children into the world. "Must be nice," Tom sniped, trundling off to work, his final year of articling. This morning he'd left early to focus on a special case.

The large man nearest the walkway looked to be asleep. He was aboriginal, his face larger than life, rearranged by a fist, perhaps, his legs too long for the bench. This much I glimpsed amid the sad miasma of the others. Curled in the fetal position, an enormous damaged crow in his filthy clothes. Folding my arms around the baby—the cautious shuffle of Gore-Tex—sleek and quick in powder blue, the same ocean paleness as the shadows cast by shrubbery, I whisked past. A lace-less workboot swung out and almost clipped me.

The morning stood out, because Tom and I had disagreed over who should get up and change the baby, fatigue pasting me to the sheets. He had early prep to do before catching his train, the firm where he was working located obtusely across town. His refrain, "You and Anna get to do whatever you want." One morning among many, it was nothing special—but I'd raced, slow as cold porridge, to get us out early, before the men from the Good Shepherd spilled from its doors.

There's something about having a purpose, an oasis: it girds you. It never occurred to me to be fearful, not after braving their gauntlet—a sort of test. Despite that foot swinging out, the men hardly moved, and in the days since Anna's birth I'd come to see them as a periphery safe-guarding the greenhouses' seclusion. Only the gainfully lonely bothered breaching it, and once wrapped in steamy solitude I never worried. I suppose you could say I felt free. The best time to come was before the crowds—other mothers, many dragging toddlers, and members of certain rare-plant societies—though most people were too busy work-ing to appear on weekdays. Their loss, for there's something about a greenhouse's full-blown abundance, the comfort of an Eden whose mildewed walls the streaming light erases.

Anna stirred. She blinked. The startled depth of a baby's eyes. The solid comfort of tiny limbs pushed against me, the still-new sensa-tion of her on the outside of my skin. Her baby grimace worked the scarf down to her chin. The perfect *o* of her mouth—don't cry, don't cry, please don't cry—settling back into a tiny rosebud. The instant we entered, the leaching warmth bathed us, against her skin piquing some recollection? I suspect it's why people flock south in winter and the crueller months of March and April, why they flee to the tropics—to remember vaguely how it was before birth, being enveloped, enclosed? Enfolded inside another's warmth.

"Land of the silver birch, home of the beaver," I hummed under my breath, the closest thing to a lullaby I knew. Going back to sleep, she gave me the unexpected bonus of more peace. In the perfect con-tentment of her body against mine, I followed miniature pathways one by one, winding past banana trees, orchids, monstrous monsteras. Stepping stones were arranged—planted amidst flaming primrose and curling pothos—as in the good witch's garden in a picture book like those whose spines had yet to be cracked, lining the white shelf that Tom, my poor harried husband, had just painted. The lushness con-jured the slither of snakes. Look up, way up—all that was missing were parakeets, cockatiels. The ripe blooms of goldfish and lipstick plants dangled, obscene against the double-glazing of ice on the roof, and through sparkling fern-patterned frost and grime, the northern sky glared blue. Babyhood memories held me: look way up—these days my own mother's voice seemed goofily at one with mine. But for Anna's straining now against my leaky breast—an infant not so different from these exotic plants craning towards sun—I was in that second deeply, raptly alone.

We *are* phototropic, I remember thinking: of course we are. Which explained Tom's choice to do law and mine to do journalism—I work as a researcher on a low-budget show investigating scams like herbal cures for cancer, erectile dysfunction, insomnia: degrees of darkness begging for some illumination.

Opening her eyes, Anna whimpered at the brightness, its filtered intensity. In their blue-brown depths was that look: Hello, milk fountain, oh one I want plugging into *now*, supplier for all my needs. But this was the first time I felt a recognition: reciprocity? She was thirteen days old. When can I take her outside? I'd asked the nurses, as if enquiring about a new, rare species, an orchid that might die being carried from shop to car. Give her a few days. Make sure she's well bundled up, and you're good to go.

"Common sense, isn't it?" said Tom. "You don't want to be stuck inside all the time." His brusqueness melded with my labour's aftershocks, those of a kind of war that happened to go well—very well, I was told. The body's urge to push replaced, replenished by gratitude—gratitude and a wild indebtedness, an impulse stronger than ever to strain and grasp at some slippery light.

So with Anna gazing up at me I savoured this moment of blissful, steamy goodness, a moment you could even call grace—till something interrupted it. A smell, a pungent odour, and the sight, beneath the spiky shade of a palm, of clothing. Dark, ragged—a pile of clothes ripe with the grief of cardboard over sidewalk vents, the eardrum-piercing shriek of subway cars below. Frostbitten fingers, toes.

The first signs of snow, I used to tell Tom when we moved in together, you feel in your fingertips: the stoniness that slows the trees' sap and kills the last geranium in its window box. Leaving our tiny flat in this grey, wintry city, he'd warm my hand in his inside his coat pocket.

Clothing, it registered, this and my first fear—arms tightening around Anna, tight tight so that her whimpers rose to that newborn's wail that makes you freeze, a-wah, a-wah, a-wah, and the milk gush. Oh our animal connection, the chafing wetness under waterproof fabric screamed, and the fear, equally animal, too. With clothes sloughed like skin from a snake, wouldn't there soon be a body going without them? Boots, one missing its sole—these registered, and a guttural, spluttering sound: aspiration. Anna was howling. The clothing shifted. A head moved.

"What the fuck!" The sour sweetness of vomit wafted, replacing that of humus and the blue ammonia scent of condensation. A battered face looked up, broken-nosed. A face bruised by darkness and want, the healing of injuries untended.

"Fuck off outta here. Ain't there nowhere a poor bastard can get some sleep?"

Something yellow leaked from the man's pants. But it was his feet that nailed my attention: soles a peaty black, filth worn into the calluses as if he'd been born with it.

"What're you gawking at, bitch? Get the fuck out, get out before a fella has to call someone."

I turned and ran. I might've unzipped my pocket, dug inside for a toonie, left it on a flagstone—but I don't remember. Anna's face was a tiny red prune: a-wah, a-wah, a-wah. She bounced in the carrier. I did remember to brace her neck with my hand. I even got her tuque back on and scarf pulled up to her nose and double-checked to find both baby mouse-sized mittens on their string and in place, all of her tucked in tight, held so close I could have worn her inside my jacket.

But she cried, and cried even harder, if that was possible, at the frigid air slamming into us. Pockmarks in the snow showed where a sprinkling of salt tried to make the walkway safer. My baby crying her head off.

The man had gotten up from his bench—the big aboriginal man in his greasy parka and floppy boots. He was shuffling towards us smoking a cigarette, hands cupping its warmth. The sun traced the tree branches' silvery melt and on the snow a sparrow hopped and pecked at a piece of donut. My eyes were on the paving stones, still icy despite the sun's climbing, the city around us fully awake now, alive. My eyes on the pathway, Anna screaming, the feel of milk soaking my shirt and the waist of my jeans. Hurry, hurry, please—if you've never had a baby, you might not know it's an APB alert when the child needs to nurse and in the face of it the world stops.

"There there little baby. There there," the man was saying.

In her frantic squirming the tuque fell off, and he stooped to pick it up. He stooped so unsteadily I was afraid, really afraid he would fall, but he didn't, and I wanted to run, run hard and catch the streetcar; and I pictured myself telling Tom later on, if I got it together enough to cook supper—because how on earth do you ever learn to function without both hands free? Without putting a child down long enough to eat and pee?

"There there, little baby." The tuque looked Disney-esque in his huge hand, the nails rimmed black, fingers stained with nicotine, that baby-poop yellow. His hand shook. It shook reaching down for Anna's head; her downy scalp, the pulsing triangle in the top of her skull where the fontanelle had barely begun to knit—a word that will always remind me of mushrooms, wild mushrooms gathered in some silent forest. As he pressed the hat down she cried, and he put his finger by her mouth. His breath was sweet like dead meat and there, there, I had it, the toonie, and I pushed it into his hand, which closed around it though he shook his head. His expression half a jeer, but pitying, gentle.

I pushed my streetcar fare at him too.

His eyes were so dark they were black. "Can I hold her?" he said.

"Are you nuts? Are you out of your fucking mind?" Tom would not sit, standing to eat the chicken I somehow managed to put in the oven. Gnawing on it while holding Anna in that awkward, slightly despairing way men have—some men, I guess I should say.

But I felt calm, calmer than I had since delivering and possibly even since learning I was pregnant. Not that any one of us knows how things will play out, falling in love with a light of our own making then refusing to imagine its hardening-off.

Who knows what the guy might do? I'd asked myself. Or what he might've done: pulled a knife, or just stumbled away? I still wonder, What if I'd refused?

He held her like a flower, a delicate flower, the kind that barely lasts a day. Her mouth the opening of a man-eating one, the cry from her lungs a little sheep's ba-a-a.

"Better get her some grub," he said, handing her back, arms bending to mine, and the greenhouses behind us sparkling, all those tropical leaves pressed to glass.

And as oddly, as awkwardly as he had entered our morning—as jarringly as any child enters the world—the man turned and, picking his way as if walking on water, disappeared into the glass house Anna and I had just left.

"It was a shelter that could have been built of ice," is what I told Tom.

BURNING TIMES

THE MOMENT THEY STEP OFF THE TRAIN THEY FEEL FOREIGN, TOO heavily Canadian in their warm dark clothes—tourists under the hazy sun, dressed not for the Tuscan spring but a Maritime one. Discombobulating, is how Keith will remember it, maneuvering their suitcases over the platform. His wife, if she cares to, will shrug off any discomfort—Cia, who gazes around hopelessly "translating" signs, realizing the best-laid plans can go awry in Italy. It's their first visit, a fifth-anniversary gift to themselves. Poor Cia—her outfit, chic at home, looks stodgily defiant. Its mummy-ish wrappings remind him of the bound chests and black T-shirts of transgender clients who come into the clinic for legal help. A complicated forgery, her dress.

The street through the grimy windows appears modern, subur-ban—neither downtown nor *quattrocento*. Cia looks at him, disgusted. This can't possibly be the right station. His fault.

"I didn't realize there was a difference."

"How could you *not*?"

He sighs with the defeat of not speaking the language. His excuses: Trenitalia's website is all in Italian, which makes bookings hit-and-miss. She shakes her head. A person waves—the only one to approach them since the Roma youth who hoisted their luggage into the overhead bin, then held out his palm, seconds before the train left Termini. The woman splays the fingers of one hand. "Another come, *cinque minuti*."

Miraculously, it does. No one checks tickets. Soon they're stepping off into Florence's central *stazione*—into the most beautiful city in the world, a Facebook friend calls it. The mistake, his mistake, rectified, all is forgiven, even the sticky, diesel-laced heat as they trundle their bags along a grimy sidewalk. A whiff of sewage—momentarily transporting him home—underwrites the perfume trailing a passerby. "So much for scent-free," Cia says, letting go of her suitcase to adjust her layers.

"The tickets to the Uffizi and the Academia are in *my* name," she reminds him, looping her purse strap over her head.

"Watch out for luggage thieves," yells a driver grabbing a smoke beside his idling bus. He kindly offers directions, holding their map upside down, drawing his thumbnail over it. Up, down, north, south— when they leave *Firenze* Keith will be no less confused about where streets lead and which way the Arno flows.

Chosen for its views—captured in pictures of the cathedral Duomo set against a pink sky (facing east, west?), of twinkling lights and bell towers framed by ancient hemlocks—the hotel isn't as it appears online. Behind the desk, the clerk has what Keith considers to be Etruscan looks—hawkish nose, narrow jaw, startling eyes—which distinguish certain Italians from others: Pinocchios from Geppettos, say. The woman's hair needs washing, her fingernails too, long and unpainted, unlike Cia's neatly filed ones and the squared-off fakes sported by others who see him for legal advice. Maybe family law wasn't his best career choice?

No matter what, the trip's a vacation from work. Cia's eyes fix on the keys behind the desk, hanging from thick leather fobs—like a Latino bike gang's regalia, she'll say, when they can laugh about it. Rows of keys and not a single one missing: full vacancy?

The ticket-sized lobby has an aged computer tucked beside a bar strung with Christmas lights. The guest book is a manila scrapbook, entries in different-coloured crayon. Guests with Russian names from Soviet-sounding places. A girls' soccer team from the U.S.—kids on a European tour. The latest entry is from a week ago, he notices, while Cia debates something with the clerk. The woman's English, though heavily accented, is quite fluent. Cia gives him the eye. Their carefully orchestrated gallery reservations have vanished in cyberspace. Whatever. He's here for the food, the wine, the history. It's Cia who's turned the trip into a pilgrimage.

"But we've come all this way—"

"No, no email. I am sorreee. I call—okay? I call." Rapid-fire Italian is exchanged over the phone. At least it's cooler and quieter in off the street, at the top of this 1950s or '60s office building in which the Hotel Panorama is accessed by a lift that seems—seemed—slightly unsafe. A smile. "For you. Special admission. Is free. Tonight, six P.M. *Si?*"

Beaming, the clerk lugs their bags up and down odd flights of stairs and along cramped corridors—like in a funhouse, a brutalist's, he thinks, the bare, greenish walls neither amusing nor carnivalesque. The "suite," no more inviting, is shown to them with a flourish. Once, it might've served as a doctor's office—seriously—all dull speckled tiles, bathroom fixtures a tired, clinical white, the tub without curtain or shower. An examination room for the leprous? Above the bed's cheap headboard, from a framed poster, Raphael's Sistine Chapel putti keep watch with glib bemusement.

Dust along the baseboards seals the atmosphere, and he feels the creep of his watered-down genes—Canadian-Scots—as if such abject austerity is penance for his being hipster-slim, red-bearded, and slightly balding where others are abundant, exuberant, especially here in this place that spawned the Renaissance. Resolutely, Cia peels off, peels away, her clothes like bandages. Testing the bathing facilities, she leaves the metal door ajar.

33

They've brought wine, slivers of pecorino cheese and prosciutto from Rome, tiny sweet tomatoes, and a bottle of pricey balsamic vinegar, which has—oh shit—leaked inside Cia's suitcase and ruined a cotton camisole. Unpacking their guidebooks, he lays out the treats on the pasteboard desk by the window. Its view of the distant Duomo is interrupted by buildings across a dingy courtyard. Turbaned in a towel, sitting on the bed, Cia accepts a plastic tumbler of Chianti. The mattress is as hard as the piazza cobbles they'll soon traverse.

They'd been warned that on the eve of a holiday rooms were scarce.

"I really couldn't tell by the photos. I mean, we could see if there's anything else."

"It's all right." Her voice is determinedly brittle, bright. "Different if we were staying more than a night."

It is a whirlwind visit and, to be truthful, the price is right; it suits their budget, Cia permanently relegated to sessional appointments, and Keith to servicing student loans. With two real incomes, he's careful not to say, Hotel Panorama wouldn't have figured in their plans. But Cia loves her work teaching Dante—the prime reason for her insisting on Florence when he'd have happily spent the week seeing ruins: Rome's Forum, the Colosseum, Octavia's Gate, the Palatine Hill where Nero supposedly fiddled while the place burned.

The room is simply somewhere to sleep, he agrees, as anxious as Cia not to spend a minute more in it than they have to.

Since Michelangelo's *David* is just around the corner—and today's reservation has been mysteriously zapped—strolling along holding hands, they decide to save it for the morning. Already it's late afternoon. They stop in a restaurant for fancy *insalatas*, a little pitcher of wine—the only diners, their voices compete with an Italian soap on TV. The taste of Gorgonzola dispels the lingering scent of powdered cleanser in their nostrils.

Negotiating block after block teeming with pedestrians, the closer they get to the Cathedral—past the outdoor market hawking "Florentine" leather knock-offs, past the fortress-like banks and *palazzos* of the Medici—the more tightly Cia clings to his arm. Roving teenagers in shorts and flip-flops grow rowdy. Like youth anywhere flaunting their ripeness, there's a loutish ease to their catcalls and shrieking laughter. It could be Pizza Corner in dowdy little Halifax. Flogging their wares, hawkers walk toy ferrets, spin flying saucers, waggle *David* statuettes. Driving the ruckus are drumbeats, distant ones—signalling a parade?

To escape, they duck into a wine shop. The friendly merchant offers a tasting, cradling in his arms a Jack Russell terrier, which gives Cia a slobbery kiss. Stroking its ears, she reminds Keith that it's almost six. They have yet to find the Uffizi, the famous Uffizi with the Botticellis she's dying to see. Travel-packing two expensive bottles—souvenirs, *si*, of our beautiful *Firenze!*—the merchant ushers them outside, closing early, he explains, because, after all, tomorrow is the first of May. Unofficially the first day of summer, a day for people to party-hearty, as you Canadians say. Keith nods. Europe's Labour Day.

"*Si, si.* To celebrate everybody, all the museums, you know, are free."

Though not particularly heavy, his purchase is unwieldy enough to make managing the throngs and holding Cia's hand impossible. Moving with the crowd they're swept along, luckily, to the huge central square—the Piazza della Signoria—where the famous gallery lies past the crenellated, bell-towered *palazzo* of the same name, and its copy of *David*. Just opposite, under an arched portico, flute players and guitarists dressed as jesters perform; their instruments' cases lean against statues—so many statues, he remarks, that after a while you stop seeing them.

They've read about the line-ups to the Galleria degli Uffizi. A coup! The queue is astonishingly short, fewer than twenty people. Cia squeezes his arm, delighted at this stroke of luck, the issue of lost bookings forgotten. But at the entrance a fresh problem arises. The sign, in French, *Inglese*, Spanish, Japanese, Russian, and Italian, prohibits umbrellas, sharp objects, food, drink—bottles of *any* kind—being brought in. An armed guard points to an overflowing bin.

Shit. *Shit.* On the fly—just arrived, a sudden crush presses impatiently at their backs—it only makes sense, Cia says: they'll take turns, visit in shifts. Since the wine is his doing, he's happy to wait and go second. He proposes a meeting place in exactly an hour. An *hour* to tour one of the world's greatest collections? The look on Cia's face is—or would be, if she weren't his wife—priceless. Someone steps on his heel; someone's lens nudges her waist. "Yep," she says.

Frankly, it's a relief to be on his own for a bit, his parcel a minor encumbrance. To think his thoughts and not have to voice them; to marvel inwardly at the marvellous and have that be sufficient. Braving a tide of gelato-slurping tourists, he passes under the museum's archway and walks along the Arno. The sun is just beginning to sink behind distant mountains which look a lot like Cape Breton's low, rounded ones. In fact, gazing downstream—or upstream?—beyond the reddish tiled rooftops he can almost see the Margaree. It *is* beautiful. Pushing, elbowing his way—*pardon, mi scusi*—he lets himself be pulled along by the crowds baby-stepping across the fairy-tale, cobbled-together jumble that's the Ponte Vecchio, past its hole-in-the-wall jewelers—their claim to fame, the guidebooks say, their having existed since the Medicis' time, gold a happy distraction from the offal dumped by butchers and tanners sharing the bridge. The very bridge, he guesses, from which the fifteenth-century heretic Savonarola's ashes were dumped after he was burned—the thanks he got for renouncing the world's vanities. Becoming fuel for a bonfire all its own when his famous ones were turned against him.

Fighting the masses to reach the opposite bank, the Oltrarno, he glimpses the bright blue message above the Uffizi's glowing windows, its neon veracity set against the sky's pale indigo: *All Art Has Been Contemporary*. It's a work, he'll find out later, by an artist he's never heard of.

Forty minutes zipped by. He cut short his stroll, any further need for solitude thwarted by sightseers tripping over each other, and hurried back to the square. The Piazza della Signoria was swollen with partiers crammed cheek to cheek, elbow to elbow, circling packs of dancers, drummers, flag-bearers and flame-throwers costumed in Renaissance velvet and silk. The lushness of red, blue, and gold was deepened and freighted by the Florentine dusk. So much for watching the sun set with Cia—Cia no doubt swooning in some vaulted, gilded room, gaga at endless depictions of madonnas, babies, and crucifixions, at Leonardo da Vinci with his "knowledge of beings" that flew "between the air and the wind."

See one religious painting and you've seen them all—not that he'd have said so.

Thunderous, the revelry around him pitched from feverish to frenzied gaiety. Drumbeats were like gunfire volleys chased by wild cheering and shouting—the crowd surging and swaying around swirling pennants and banners, the dizzying swaths these cut through the masses. The hawkers' glow-in-the-dark doodads rose and spun overhead, the wobbling rings of made-in-China Saturns. Drunk on cheer, the intoxicated teetered toward debauchery—a scene that was vaguely threatening, all the more so for being incomprehensible.

Raising his elbows, hugging the wine to his chest, he managed to shove his way through tangled humanity across the square, where, in the shadow of fake *David*, Cia had agreed to meet. Okay, so one hour in the Uffizi was a little unfair. But wasn't the whole trip a compromise, squeezing in as much as they could? Someday they'd return: there's always a next time.

The evening had cooled considerably, a tangy chill coming off the river, and he regretted leaving behind his sweatshirt, wrapped as it was around a jar of tapenade in his suitcase and the little Bernini figurine he'd bought for Cia, to surprise her with at dinner. Their anniversary was in three days, to be celebrated in Venice if all unfolded as expected—if anything could be expected in a country where craziness ruled and still the trains ran, impeccably, on time. Now *that* was mysterious.

Underlying the sharp breeze, the sewage smell wafted again, a reminder of the need to suspend, dispel, feelings of undue romance and diffidence.

But where *was* she? It was twenty minutes past the appointed time, and still no sign of her. Reluctantly they'd left the phone they shared charging in the room. Twenty minutes became forty. He hadn't moved;

dared not stray a foot from the spot. But, shoving in to pose for selfies under *David*'s massive genitals, a pack of teenagers forced him to meld with the mob's fringes churning toward the middle of the square. All he could see of the pageantry were the peaks of celebrants' caps, the hawkers' spinning toys helicoptering through the air.

After an hour and still no sign of her, he wondered if Cia too had got caught in the swell and stranded in some other, unlikely location. Looking down—the only way to keep steady was by gazing at his shoes—he found himself planted on a round metal plaque naming Fra Girolamo Savonarola and two other *fras*, a date in Roman numerals. The site of the famous conflagrations, the monk's Bonfires of the Vanities, where he had burned books, mirrors, and paintings not "of God" before he was torched. Even Botticelli himself was thought to have willingly tossed a canvas or two to the flames, the artist Cia would gush about when she appeared. *If* she appeared—where the heck was she? By now a full hour and a half had lapsed.

Annoyance—a sharp impatience, a heated indignation—filled him. The musicians had long disappeared, defeated by the drumbeats ricocheting from walls and crenellated roofs, punching their deafening holes in the sky. The crush staggered and reeled. Skulking hawkers began to fling and bundle trinkets into blankets, weary, perhaps, of their own preying and pleading.

Dread descended, a bloat of worry and fear. Squeezing between leering drunks he found the museum's exit, where a guard was hustling people outside. He tried asking if the fellow had seen her—the drumming as relentless as shelling—then loitered the ten minutes till closing time.

She'd got lost, was struggling to find her way to the hotel?

It was two hours past their meeting time. He pushed his way to the museum's entrance, now locked. The guard behind the glass, who'd overseen the pitching of umbrellas and bottled water, barely shrugged.

She'd hailed a cab, got back on her own steam, and now, in a panic, awaited him? But no, *no*, she wouldn't have done that, gone off alone, left him hanging.

Two and a half hours past, the unthinkable stalked him.

She'd done this on purpose. She was leaving—she *had* left: had dragged him across the ocean and how many time zones and up and down how many *vias* and *calles* to silently give him the slip?

He thought of finding a policeman, getting directions to the police station. What would he say? A missing person. *What, your wife, she go shopping? She get hungry, she go find some pasta?* His head pounded. Each drumbeat usurped his heart's: an invasion. And meanwhile the frenzy would continue till, what, dawn? Till one by one, the revellers dropped to the cobblestones, exhausted?

He pictured her cabbing to the airport, flashing her passport, her credit card.

His stomach grumbled. His ears ached. He shivered, the wind off the Arno now bitter. She'd dumped him. Five years of his life, their lives— as good as clothes, photos, and furniture thrown onto a pyre and lit.

He pictured himself riding the rattling, shaking elevator up to the room, crawling between chilly, sour-smelling sheets. Almost without his noticing, a dusky blackness had settled over the square, the sky barely punctuated by stars—what stars were visible suddenly enviable for their distance. Dumped. He'd been dumped.

Along the clogged street down which they'd gambolled by daylight— jostling elbows, holding on to each other, laughing—artisans lined the dark sidewalk selling pottery and wooden carvings now barely visible. As he started to cross to the other side, something snagged his sleeve.

"Hey! Where's the fire?" She was laughing, peering up at him, craning for a kiss. Her face was pale and round and happy. Looping her arm through his—"Keith? What's wrong?"—she was shouting—"You look like you've seen a Medici ghost. What's your problem?"

"Where the *fuck* were you?" was all he could think to say.

The tense walk to the hotel—not a cab to be seen or a stretch of pavement clear enough to accommodate one—allowed only this:

"I waited three hours. As long as one of your fucking classes."

"I lost track of time. Know what? Up close the waves in *Venus* look like birds done by preschoolers."

"I thought you'd died. I was—I thought—"

"Do you realize how *fast* an hour goes, standing in front of a da Vinci?"

"I thought you'd left me."

"Well I didn't. Haven't—yet—have I."

Lying together in the bed, careful that his back didn't touch hers, he felt his anger settle to a slow, slower, burn, sensing hers: it was bright, fierce and hateful.

But the sun rose on Florence, beautiful Florence. Not speaking, they found themselves together in the breakfast room, the only ones beside a Slavic-looking couple snapping pictures of each other.

What a disappointment, the breakfast. It was laughable: plastic tablecloths, vending machines dispensing Froot Loops and instant cappuccino.

Sitting there, they let their hands creep closer, then touch, paging silently through guidebooks, each to a fresco on the Oltrarno: Masaccio's *Adam and Eve* skulking away from Paradise, grief-stricken, banished.

"The Academia opens in half an hour."

"If we hurry, we can cross the river too, then get back for the train."

Packing up first, Cia wrapped the expensive vinegar in a plastic bag, placed the ruined camisole in the wastebasket beneath the sink. He found room in his bag for the wine. Weighing convenience against better judgment, they left both suitcases to be retrieved just before checkout time.

The ugliness on poor Eve's face made the race across the Ponte Vecchio and back more than worthwhile, even he had to admit.

Before grabbing their bags, he says he'll meet her downstairs, pleading the need for a quick, final pit stop. "Going once, going twice, Cia? Last chance to sit on the Panorama's throne."

She promises, with a roll of the eyes, to wait in the lobby, not to go anywhere.

In the bare-bones bathroom—the sun streaming through pebbled glass lighting porcelain dull as old teeth—he unpacks the Bernini figurine. It's an impromptu purchase he'd made on impulse in Rome, in an upscale souvenir shop in Prati, because they had missed seeing the real thing—maybe next year?

Representing a god groping a nymph, its molded plastic was meant to resemble marble. It *is* a little tacky; no, more than that, it is straight-up cheesy.

But his heart had been in the right place buying it—yes, it had. At the time.

This much he feels sure of, enfolding it in the camisole and leaving it for the chambermaid.

if MY FEET DON'T TOUCH *the* GROUND

BERLIN IS A CITY OF *PIETÀS*, OF HARD GOODBYES—BUT PERCHED high above Mitte drinking wine, I lock out the thought, let it drop like a useless key to the courtyard many stories below. By some fluke we have the balcony all to ourselves—it wraps around the entire top floor—the hotel gods, the gods of hospitality, having blessed us? Jet-lagged, woozy, we toast Christopher, his father and I no less blissful than the day our son was born, no less stunned by the ease with which certain things work out: the crush of connecting flights forgotten, our year-long separation—the length of Chris's absence— is today erased.

It's a balmy April evening; the air has a blush. Our laughter sweetens the birdsong that fills it; we can't see them but we can hear them, a multitude of birds, as if there's one on every railing, every rooftop, every tree. The scent not of currywurst but of blossoms drifts up from the courtyard's garden, once a square of pavement divided by the Wall. A hot-air balloon bearing a map of the globe and the newspaper logo *Die Welt*, hikes itself closer to the peach-coloured sun. Our mood is just as weightless. There will be no tears. Gil and I and Christopher will make these days together last. We'll apply hard brakes against their ending, sure; for now, feeling unbroken joy in such a city seems slightly akin to gloating.

"Danka*shun*,"—Chris elbows his dad, topping up his own glass— "that's 'thank you *very* much.'"

He is the same but different: thinner, definitely, sporting a gauntness that matches his Hitler *jugend*-style fade. His Berliner's lisp is just for fun, but its softness genuine. It draws us more tightly around the little glass-topped table, no one but the dive-bombing swallows to overhear.

"Say 'excuse me,' again. One more time."

"*Entschuldigung.* Ent-shool-d'goong." His laugh is patient, wry, worldly as any twenty-five-year-old's.

Breathing a moment's silence, we drink in our surroundings: the glass façades of sleek new architecture briefly tinted coral. Except for the language, we could be in Toronto. But any street sounds are too remote to catch—odd, because Mitte means the middle of things, the street we're on, Schützenstrasse, once demarking West from East. It's a pigeon's hop from Checkpoint Charlie, and mere steps from the museums remembering victims of the secret police and of the Nazis, the outdoor Topography of Terror set in the Gestapo's ruins.

"You should check them out," Chris says, that worldliness again. "I haven't been yet—no time. Really, I'm not too into this stuff. Nobody here is." He mentions some Canadian dude recently busted for going 'heil' outside the Reichstag. "Hitler's just not something you bring up, you know? So, don't go dropping the H-bomb, okay?" Classic Chris: he's kidding, and he's not.

Putting out snacks, Gil smiles. "We're here to see *you*."

There's so much to catch up on since he left home with a backpack, not even taking along an instrument.

Guitarist of a thousand licks, no longer the plaid- and tuque-wearing indie kid he was when he left Halifax, he pulls on the grey cashmere coat he was wearing to meet us at Tegel, says he'll see us in the morning.

⌐ ⌐ ⌐

It's not ideal waking up slightly hungover on your first full day in a foreign city, having your husband snap a photo of you by a chunk of Wall while skirting sites of past horrors. But by the time Chris meets us, at a café near Checkpoint Charlie, I'm pretty much recovered, back in bliss mode.

Are we really together, Chris and Gil and I, sidestepping the sandbagged garden-shed piece of Cold War America meant to jog a tourist's pulse?

"No pictures—not *here*." Chris is adamant, until we stumble across Oldenburg's *Houseball*, a giant dust bunny of a sculpture, its displaced chairs, buckets, ladders, and mops done in playground colours that entice Chris to pose, dwarfed by it—this boy of ours once the architect of Duplo castles, light on his feet as seafoam, racing waves at the beach. I shoot a zillion pictures of him in his elegant coat, a perk, we hear, from a recent gig. A good thing he lets me, because next stop is the Memorial to the Murdered Jews of Europe and its aisles and aisles, block upon block, of steles grey as tombstones—2,710 of them in all, says the guidebook, a number as random yet calculated as the deaths they mark. A measure of evil's way of swamping then feeding on banality, they mount in height as our child leads the way. He melds with them, all but vanishing into grey.

The soft brown of his half-shaved head, the pink of his neck and hands are the only living colours. These and a narrow plank of blue above and a needle's eye of green ahead—leaves in bud—draw us through.

Sunlight and ivy lace the barbed-wire voids in this beautiful city with a lushness and manicure all their own, nature's tempered resilience. At the Brandenburg Gate, Chris takes our picture, then Gil takes Chris and me together, our son's smile hovering, and mine showing the wear and tear of a Maritime excuse for spring. But under its surface happiness chugs, the Little Engine That Could: the resolve to want, to expect, nothing more.

From there we circle the Reichstag, visit Museum Island, stroll Unter den Linden, where the evil one razed its eponymous trees the better to parade troops. There, in a guardhouse all its own, stands Käthe Kollwitz's *Mother with her Dead Son*—the work of a woman who lost her boy to the First World War and a grandson to the Second, so I read from the guidebook. The mother enfolds the corpse in heavy arms as if her warmth might breathe life back into the body. We tiptoe around her bearing her grief, the three of us in the eye of it, silent.

Because a certain stopwatch has begun to tick: our stay is far too short, it dawns. He has rehearsals, he says—no mention yet of the girl, woman, he'd travelled with who recently left. He has meetings with immigration people, he tells us. Meetings with a manager, the son of a prince who once booked Bob Dylan's tours, he says. There's talk of a trip to Majorca. The band is a group of guys he met on Craigslist, upper-crust expat Brits. Wanted: guitar & keys player, backup singer. He's applied for an artist's visa, hopes to stay.

It's a very long way from Halifax, garage rock in our basement.

As the sun sinks, we head back to the hotel to picnic on treats. I could hole up forever in this room. It has two of everything—queen-size beds, sofas, bathrooms—its luxury all the more luxurious because it's not what we booked.

"Still have that Les Paul?" Chris asks Gil, cracking beers.

"Ever find out what happened to your Fender?" Chris's favourite guitar, one Gil shipped that disappeared at a show but was mysteriously replaced by another worth three times as much.

"Like I told you, the room was locked."

The talk darkens. We debate evil's roots, as people can and do in a hotel room high above clean modern streets.

"Everyone has it in them to do like the Nazis did," Chris says fiercely. Pointing out Al-Qaeda, Rwanda, Bosnia, what the Brits did to the Mi'kmaq and the Beothuks, for Chrissake. It's not as if such madness has limits, what happened in Germany "just" a confluence.

"You're right," Gil hedges. "Plenty of Hitlers—history's full of them. Look at Stalin."

"But how could so many people follow such an obvious nutcase?" Ordinary, normal ones, I mean, not the Goebbels, Goerings, Eichmanns, Himmlers, and Speers.

"People will do whatever they have to, to save their own skin."

He enfolds me in a hug before heading to the U-Bahn, bound for the drummer's flat—the place that, for now, he calls home.

Chris is busy the next day. Gil and I stick together, our feet taking us along Zimmerstrasse, where we vowed not to go. The Stasi exhibition has acid-green rooms, a Cold War rolodex with hundreds of thousands of names, people tracked by the secret police, people executed for wanting to vote. One hundred and eleven kilometers of documents and 1.4 million photographs document the price of freedom to come and go, says the leaflet. Chills worm from my shoulders to my stomach, but with nothing but time we push on, passing a place that rents out psychedelic Ladas by the hour and another offering *Die Welt* balloon rides. Across from a block-long stretch of Wall grimly intact, we hurry through the Topography of Terror, then up Wilhelmstrasse past Goebbels's two-thousand-room Ministry of Aviation, one of very few such edifices not razed after the war.

I need Tylenol and art, more art.

The afternoon crawls by. Finding ourselves in leafy, bourgeois Charlottenburg—where, according to Chris, no one goes—we enter a garden dotted with statues, the chill, gracious solitude of a house that would fit in the finest of Parisian neighbourhoods. The museum's a monument to Kollwitz, champion of the proletariat, who gave her life to depicting poor parents—maker of *pietàs* and "degenerate" art, as Hitler called it—bereaved mother and wife of a Prenzlauer Berg doctor as working class as a doctor could be. Apart from a couple of women whispering in German, we're the only visitors. The sketches and prints on the walls are one long tortured cry against violence and hate, the poverties of spirit that sever all physical bonds—yet the pictures whisper a hard, stoic love that outlives time, place, and gunfire.

We find that neither of us can speak. It's never good tearing up, let alone weeping, in public, and we're forced by genteel circumstances to flee. I'm no shopper but manage to buy a poster of *The Sacrifice*. Its desperate mother offers a newborn out of turmoil's darkness into light—the child itself her only hope. A souvenir from this part of Berlin where, our child insists, artists never go.

Choosing what seems a gentler, friendlier route back to the hotel, we follow a green canal, then stumble upon what's left of the last station many—most?—Jews saw before the one at Auschwitz.

Just before dusk Chris comes to take us on a stroll through Kreuzberg, in and out of tiny galleries teeming with all kinds of art from all around the globe. We sign petitions demanding Ai Weiwei's release from a Chinese prison. A group swathed in red latex—red rubber Buddhas?—performs a silent outdoor dance, and around a pond near Oranienstrasse chestnuts bloom, wisteria and lilacs, and in the settling dark a sprinkling of tiny daisies makes a Milky Way of the grass. A form of resistance, the flowers' quiet won't be crushed. It's cooler tonight. Carrying food from a Turkish grocer's, we race back to our rooftop haven, keen to put our feet up. But a restlessness stirs in us—I can almost hear it—our time in Berlin half over and Chris soon departing, disappearing up Friedrichstrasse.

When Gil and I wake, it's the sixty-sixth anniversary of the H-monster's suicide deep inside the bunker buried now under a car park and some Soviet-era apartments. Blink and you'll miss the sign giving its location— and we almost do. But could it be that evil's molecules hang around, that the air the psychopath breathed still exists? What's become invisible explains why my father's generation crossed the ocean to fight this enemy. It's my father's face I see in Chris's—especially in publicity shots he's shown us, of the band wearing shirts and ties under their pricey coats. Let's leave history buried, Gil and I decide, buying chocolate. It fortifies us for today's walk to Prenzlauer Berg, where they rehearse.

Crossing Karl-Marx-Allée, lured by greenery, we get lost in an overgrown graveyard whose entrance is the only exit. All the headstones are dated 1945—the year the city surrendered to the Russians and Hitler ate cyanide, or whatever—and bear Jewish names and Christian crosses. Walking in circles, panicking, eventually we free ourselves in time to find Greifswalder Strasse and Chris waiting on a corner.

We're all early, and stop to buy drinks to kill time in Berlin's oldest park. Chris nudges me past the entrance—"You've got to see this, Mom"—to the Märchenbrunnen fountain where every imaginable fairy tale figure stands in pure white marble. Little Red Riding Hood, Cinderella, Snow White, Sleeping Beauty, Hansel and Gretel. Placed for the pleasure of children when typhoid and rickets ruled, these gentle creations survived endless bombings *and* Soviet rule. Just beyond them, we lie on the grass at the foot of a steep slope, sip and talk, and he and Gil doze. Like father, like son.

Volkspark Friedrichshain looks and feels like Central Park. But its hills—*bunkerbergs*—are made of rubble, all that was left of this city after the war.

Sitting up, Chris eyes his watch.

The rehearsal space is at the bottom of a gulag-style building, through an abandoned underground parkade and a barely lit warren of graffiti-tagged passages full of trash: signs of habitation, a squat? What interrogations happened here before the Wall fell, I wonder: not artistic ones. Through a series of steel doors we finally enter the studio's antechamber, a tiny space with toilet, fridge, chairs and table, and a Rage Against the Machine poster with nuns pointing rifles. The inner sanctum is a cell jammed with gear, carpeting growing up the walls, dangling pipes and wires.

The guys are warming up. They're sweet, polite, welcoming—even the wild-eyed upholsterer filling in for the bassist who's taken a job in publishing. Chris plugs in. They're practically reverential.

When they play, the music blows the space apart, tears it open. It's re-channeled, re-charged U2, well-seasoned and steeped in electropop.

Don't say it; keep the comparisons to yourself, Mom, say Chris's eyes glancing up from the fretboard, ready to roll themselves at any second. Beyond commercially viable and tighter than Gil and I could have imagined, the song—"Why Am I So Holy?"—is all that's tireless in this city, and burns through soundproof walls. Chris's guitar makes it. We've heard him play thousands of times, of course; these guys have taken him on the strength of his earlier work. When they break, they make politely envious jokes about his youth, his skinniness.

Gil is pale; he has to get outside, get some air, escape this subterranean place. The look in his eyes is all deer-in-the-headlights. He can't speak. Normally an ambler, he marches in total silence all the way past the misbegotten graveyard, past Karl-Marx-Allée, barely nodding at more gulag-style buildings and happy-worker murals peeling from dead apartment blocks. It's not till we've passed the Fernsehturm, that Soviet-style CN Tower, that words start to come, and not far from here, near a bend in the Spree, that we happen upon our second *pietà*. Nameless, she sits near the ruins of a church, her limbs ramrod straight, her son's body laid over her lap: an intersection of hard lines that defy human comfort.

"Chris *should* be here," Gil finally says. "He needs to be here, he needs to stay in Berlin."

He invites us for drinks. The drummer and his girlfriend throw a dinner party in our honour. The talk is of childhoods spent in European boarding schools. The lead singer asks what we think of the latest royal wedding. They debate a new name for the band. Chris proposes The Junior Bengal Lancers, after the riding stable back home. They love it. Post-post colonialism at its best?

On our last day we meet again in Prenzlauer Berg. Another rehearsal. The band goes on tour tomorrow, a circuit of German cities. A photographer arrives to do a shoot; there's a meeting with a videographer, talk of recording in London, a CD to be released in the fall—copies of which our son will deal like cards at the dinner table next Christmas. This time Gil and I are more composed. We listen coolly from the outer room, under the blank, identical faces of the gun-toting nuns.

Today's music is loud, driving, and every bit as tight as yesterday's. But there's a sameness, I find, a tiredness even, that escaped me before, though it still sinks a now-familiar hook into my chest.

The Berlin spring turns cold that evening, a frigid wind driving the three of us to seek comfort food. Our last supper, who knows for how long? The restaurant, where sparkling wine was invented, has an unappealing menu, at least in translation: lukewarm potato salad, beef brisket. The kind of stuff that sticks in your throat. My wiener schnitzel blankets the plate, the size and shape of an Egyptian neckpiece like those in the Altes Museum. Chris's guitarwork still sears my hearing. I have never tasted finer food, yet can barely swallow.

Don't cry, *don't.*

The hours, the minutes count down to goodbye.

Don't waste them. Don't.

Back in the hotel room, gathered around one TV, the three of us attempt the last-ditch, inane chitchat when there's too much of one thing and not enough of another to say.

It is as if we'll never see him again. As if the present, even as it's happening, is remote from us, already irretrievable.

The only English channel, besides some porn ones, is rerunning a Rock and Roll Hall of Fame reunion, the stars of our youth—Gil's and mine—taking the stage. Springsteen, Jagger, Crosby, Stills and Nash. Some are shipwrecks. Others have chins, arches, and other parts that haven't quite so visibly gone south. Gil and Chris zero in on guitar makes. I fixate on the costumes, the makeup, the gaudy decrepitude: one way of warding off the evil tears.

Debonair, Jeff Beck rocks a muscle shirt, grandfatherly arms quivering with each vibrato—as Gil's would, and mine too, if I played. But the rock in my chest is a *bunkerberg*, the sting behind my eyes pure pins and needles.

"Mutton dressed as lamb," I say, strategically. This is what we do, fighting back.

"Saw him back in '71," says Gil. "Suffers from tinnitus, you know. Great guitar player, especially when he played with Clapton. Underappreciated, obviously. Loves his Les Pauls."

"Remember the time some guy phoned looking for your Left Paw?" Our ancient, foolproof joke falls flat. Chris just stares at the TV.

Next up is Black Sabbath, or their remains. Today *is* a black Sabbath; it couldn't be blacker, says Gil's look. Just as the tears tingle, Ozzy Osbourne's doughy face fills the screen. "Let's go fucking wild," he screams, "go fucking crazy," and launches into that troglodytic dirge of an anthem, "Iron Man." The camera pans the shrieking, fist-pumping audience, then settles on him. With his dyed hair and eyeliner he looks for all the world like a woman you'd see back home at the No Frills, pushing a grocery cart full of squirming grandchildren. Out of my mouth this pops; judgmental, yes, but true enough to draw a chuckle. Chris shakes his head. Gil gapes at the screen. The *bunkerberg* in the room has taken on an icy form, large enough to sink something.

By now the tears are backing up, air bubbles in a hose. When they finally break loose they spill down—with glee. I've always hated metal, its mullets and wristbands, not to mention its sound. Laughter cracks me open. It cracks each of us open, a chain reaction. "That *is* how he looks." Gil is choking.

"You *guys*." But Chris is laughing too.

The three of us sprawl in a slew of tears and delight and the whole crazy recognition of joy and grief, how tightly entwined they are, a tangled, messy dustball. I've always hated Ozzy Osbourne. But tonight Ozzy is king, Ozzy is spectacle: the god of rock and roll and all that matters, which right now is laughter, and more laughter. I could watch him for the rest of my life, letting everything in me spill.

We're laid out by our laughter, helpless, a howling little trinity.

All too soon it's over. Ozzy blows kisses: "I love you fuckers!" If he weren't here beside me, I'd offer my child to Ozzy in thanks. If I could, I'd reach through the screen and squeeze his pudgy hand. But then he leaves the stage and the cheering fizzles, and it's time.

We put our boy in a cab, blowing kisses. The paleness of his face, his palm raised in a wave, and the driver's vague smile are what we carry with us to bed, and for months and months afterwards.

"Are they your parents?" the driver said.

We wake to the news that Osama Bin Laden is dead. My treasure in tow—the cheap, matted repro of Kollwitz's *Sacrifice*—we catch our early morning flight to Rome.

The band records the last single of its career in Berlin that summer, a piece of Emo-electropop titled "Feet Won't Touch The Ground." Soon after, its members disband to "move in new directions"—and Chris returns in time for winter, to cool his itchy feet in Halifax before they take him off again, to Toronto this time: city of his birth, city of new dreams.

The song isn't the music he made ages ago in our basement or at the Pavilion or the Rock Garden, or even in that gulag cavern in Greifswalder. The CD's best feature is the cover art: a black and white photo of Chris from the neck down—white shirt, narrow waist, snake hips, impossibly skinny jeans, and boots—shot against a monumental emptiness.

It's a runway at Tempelhof, he tells me: archetype of Nazi delusions, an airport terminal built in the 1930s to serve their "world capital"—the seed of Hitler's wildest aspirations. Still one of Europe's biggest buildings, abandoned just a few years ago, it was used by Berlin's occupiers after the war to airdrop food to the starving, candy to children.

By a trick of Photoshop our boy levitates, hovering just above the surface of its infinite tarmac.

the GROTTO

BRAKES JUDDERING, THE COACH LURCHED AND SWAYED THROUGH sun-drenched streets, gears gnashing as it lumbered uphill. Stomachs swayed with it, gazes leapfrogging, the view a dazzling terracotta blur: shuttered houses, flowers storming balconies. "Lour*des*," burbled the driver, throwing his weight behind the last syllable, "duh," like a teenager would say. Tilley-hatted heads craned, Yankee accents yammered. So much easy-care polyester it wasn't funny. Gulping bottled water, fighting nerves, despite the air-conditioned chill Arlene sweated impatience. Had Em been there ("duh!") she'd have got them kicked off for making snide remarks—snotty Canucks!—this the only tour that would eventually, please, yes, take her to Font-de-Gaume.

Or so she'd understood it was—her French not up to quibbling with the ticket agent in Toulouse—till she found herself heading southwest, not northeast. But, everything being new, she told herself, it was all good. Except she only had the week, and now this useless stop before they looped back up to the Dordogne and the cave paintings she'd travelled all this way to see. A good four hours from where she wanted to be, the last place on earth she'd choose to visit, the very last, was a Catholic shrine—a believer's Disneyland. "A place of miraculous cures," said the guidebook. Not a crutch or rosary to be seen among her fellow passengers—this was one good sign, maybe the only one, a reassurance. Still the Beatles's "Magical Mystery Tour" rolled through her head as they ground to a halt.

Everyone stood. Letting others push ahead, she watched them spill across the parking lot. Women, the odd husband in tow, reasonably hale for their age—and no obvious fanatics. Em, who dressed like the homeless, would've called her judgmental for that. But any self-reproach lifted as she waved someone on, a man she hadn't noticed boarding. Where had he come from, grinning at her? But then she'd been a little distracted, agitated was more like it. "Age before beauty," she heard. Not till they'd disembarked—the bus's cool laced with a burning smell exchanged now for a slam of sticky heat—did she notice he had a walker.

Inside the grim little hotel was equally sweltering. Queuing for the toilet she let others go ahead of her—pity those weak-bladders; don't cause a stir, even when entitled to. She imagined Em doing a pee dance, how she would have charged ahead.

Relief that the stop wasn't overnight buzzed up and down the following queue, a line-up for the dining room, a space partially redeemed by its view. Rooftops spread below, the colour of sundried tomatoes in a deep green bowl, the surrounding hills under a yellow haze. Fanning herself—her brochure flashing pictures of azure skies—a woman nudged Arlene. "Y'all travelling by your lonesome? We're stuck here for *sank* hours—we're *paying* for this?"

Salad was all the buffet offered by the time a spot came available, next to the fellow who'd spoken on the bus. Sipping wine, he was fiddling with an expensive-looking camera. Nice hands, she thought, even if they showed a certain hesitance. His crisp outdoor adventure-style clothes seemed at odds with the walker. A wife, a partner to match would soon appear? But patting the plastic seat— "It's got your name on it"—he flagged someone down to bring more water.

Hennigan was his name, Michael. He came from Toronto, she heard, helping herself to the last croissant in its plastic basket. His forthrightness was cheering. It made her think of someone back home, a professor who taught a course having to do with Pavlov's dogs. Typing up his memos, her interest wasn't necessarily feigned.

"Don't know about you, but I'm here to get healed." Hennigan grinned as he spoke. His laugh was robust. "Dessert?" Before she could offer to go for some, leaving his camera and pristine-looking daypack, maneuvering the walker, he returned with two acid-yellow tarts. While she was getting coffee the driver appeared and shouted mostly in French. The bus had a problem, a mechanical issue, it seemed. Not to worry, a replacement was being found, though their ETA in the Dordogne would be delayed: "*À huit heures*, at the latest." Up went a solitary cheer—"More time to visit Our Lady!"—the rest of the announcement drowned out by groans.

"*Quelle surprise.*" Hennigan made her think again of the Pavlovian, who'd been making noises recently about dinner at the faculty club. "Sorry—I didn't catch your name," he said, though she was sure she'd told him. Offering his hand, he gave hers a businesslike grip. She repeated her name, her married one—Deveau—kept for Em's sake, she explained, and no, she didn't speak French but wished she could; a little embarrassed, not wanting to seem stupid, she didn't explain.

"So you have a daughter." His smile was quizzical, touchingly so. "You miss her?"

"Just a bit." She made a point of ignoring the walker, its flipped-down seat shelving his belongings. Its metallic red seemed better suited to a muscle car. Only his thinness—accentuated by his greying hair, wire-rimmed glasses, and wrinkle-free pants—and the hint of a tremor in his hands suggested infirmity. He was clearly travelling alone, and not averse to visiting this tourist trap, angling for help? It crossed her mind.

Outside, the bus sat with its engine off. Hennigan looped his camera strap over his head. Dizzying sunlight bounced from clay and stucco.

She pressed her palm against the hotel's prickly shaded wall, savouring an illusion of coolness. A minor glitch, this; soon they'd be under-way—though in just two days her flight home left Paris. The thought made her queasy again; she wasn't the most adventurous traveller. But the dancing brightness flooded the street swarming with visitors and, washing cloudless blue and the Pyrenées's snowy peaks in its glow, snubbed her worries.

"Up for a hike?" Hennigan eyed her dressy sandals. Her running shoes were stowed, naturally, deep aboard the bus. They wouldn't be going far, it seemed fairly obvious.

"As long as we stick to the streets."

In the distance below, a dull green river threaded past clus-tered buildings. High on a hill beyond it, some ruins—a castle, some ancient fortification?—blended mirage-like with their rocky perch. She could already feel a blister starting, but the sight took her mind off it. The ruins reminded her of Em, tiny Em playing a fairy princess, her daddy's little girl.

Busily snapping photos, Hennigan was unaccountably spry. The steep little street soon gave way to a human river sweeping them along. Exactly what she'd vowed never to do after the divorce: let herself be swept up or steered. She could've stayed at the hotel to nurse a drink; wasn't that the trouble with travelling alone, the pos-sibility of multiple choices? Not that having too many choices was a problem. While flying across the ocean, flying into the sun, loneliness had pricked her, not out of missing Em but, unaccountably, her ex. A reflex, the psych professor would've said; and nothing a miniature bottle of wine didn't ease.

Just as soothing, if not exactly comforting, was how well Hennigan knew his way. Not that a person could get badly lost here: the pluses of a hilly place, so many vantage points. Her toe started to ooze, but forgetting it, forgetting herself, she pointed out a spire jutting above the rooftops. Hennigan set the walker's brakes while he focused his lens.

At the foot of the hill the streets were a warren clogged with sightseers. Dusty shop-fronts teemed with souvenirs—crucifixes, figu-rines of Virgin Mary and a little grey nun that made Arlene think of a toy penguin Em had cherished. Cramming the windows with a dreary repetition, so many tiny hands clasped in prayer, the miniature nuns cast pious eyes upwards. *Little Saint Bernadette*, said cardboard signs penned in English, *patron of the hopelessly ill.*

Her toe was now bleeding. Hennigan pressed on, his tanned face a bit flushed, the limp that she'd soon noticed only slightly pronounced. "*Pauvre petite* Bernadette,"—he patted his chest, grimacing good-naturedly—"see what happens when the capitalist spirit runs amok?"

"And isn't religion just that, exploiting the lame?" Even if rehearsed, more or less the professor's view, it came out rather harshly, no hope of being retracted.

"No one does kitsch better than Cat'licks."

Rummaging for her phone—curse this oversized purse—she went to take a picture. Em would approve. But it was dead, the charger packed with her sneakers, of course. She had to hurry to catch up, red smearing her sandal strap. Hennigan was mopping his temples, which offered some satisfaction. "You know exactly where you're going, I take it." She didn't mean to sound sarcastic.

He'd been here before, oh yes, years ago, with his wife who had died—died much too young, he said, eyeing her—of cancer. Looking away politely, she fixed on the crowds pushing past. "It happened after I was diagnosed myself. With MS, multiple sclerosis." His voice was matter-of-fact, as if he knew what she was thinking: false hope, the last resort of those desperate and crazy enough to come to such places seeking "cures." Hype and hocus-pocus, the weak being preyed on because of their faith. Following a god that heaped suffering on suffering, the reward for faith more suffering—what could be more foolish? Drooling dogs pressing keys in order to get fed, learned behaviour a reflex: *this* made sense.

"My illness? No big deal, till lately," Hennigan said, as if he owed her the explanation. "A bit of a limp, a little numbness was all."

Her smile was meant to be encouraging, if a bit disengaged. Grit from the cobbles worsened her own complaint, the blister a tiny misery. Be grateful, she told herself, and of course she was.

"At least the souvenirs are from China and not pieces of saints."

"Relics? You'd take plastic over the real thing? That Catholic penchant for cadaverous tissue. Squeamish, are we?"

"Dead bones and skin—they're supposed to prove something? I can't think what. Isn't it all a little"—she searched for the prof's word, the correct one—"anthropophagic?"

"Like saying someone's a little pregnant?" Hennigan laughed, clearly enjoying this—though he leaned on the walker, less an accessory now than a necessity? "A priest I know buys relics on eBay. His mission, rescuing them from profiteers."

"Cannibal collectors?" A bad joke, which she regretted.

"You've been to Italy? Something we saw in a cathedral, once—my wife and I. An entire skeleton in a tiny glass casket like Snow White's."

"How tiny?" It was what Em would've asked.

"Jewelry box–size, maybe. A feat of compression, I'm telling you."

"Whose, um, was it? Not that it matters."

"Saint Clement's maybe? Or just some guy's. Lost to me now, I'm afraid. At the time we hardly cared." His smile was half embarrassed, yet in the heat it shimmered the way the streets did—streets such a maze that the two of them could've been lab rats.

Petering out, the shops gave onto a plaza crowded with people. A rushing sound rose above their thrum, and beyond a motorcade of wheelchairs Arlene glimpsed glinting green and a bridge bleached white by the glare. Crossing it, they dodged a multitude limping along on crutches and conveyances as spiffy as the Mars Rover. The able-bodied plunged past: nuns in Nikes, couples spearing their way along with Nordic hiking poles. Speed-walkers and cripples alike, humanity log-jammed then spilled around a diapered man lying on the cobbles, his grotesquely clubbed foot on display. She looked gently past the outstretched arm, the empty cup.

Hennigan eyed the sluicing current. "I mean to put that off as long as possible." He could've meant anything by it: taking the future into his hands and leaping, or stooping to some vague yet certain indignity? Reasserting itself, her queasiness must have shown. "You're a long way from Nova Scotia. What really brings you here?" His voice was earnest, but his eyes were teasing. "Not to France, but this holiest of places."

"My sub-par French?" She imagined Em elbowing her. *Don't be so fucking lame.* "An accident, trust me—nothing more. Next time I'll—" Be up-front, forthright, especially around believers: fanatics, the ignorant, the professor said, had ways of ganging up. Not that Hennigan struck her as being either—a bit presumptuous maybe, but gently so. As for belief, the only time in her life she'd even imagined praying was at the end of the marriage, and then mainly for Em's sake.

A boy with a snake tattoo squeezed by, and she pictured the barbed wire bracelet inked around her daughter's wrist.

"I'll admit, there can be something off-putting about all this. People in such need." Hennigan slung his pack over his shoulder, wincing. "I know none of it makes much sense. Time to sit, I'm afraid." Perched on his movable seat, he mimicked a couple of old men seated on a bench, canes hooked over their knees. Yet his languor seemed youthful, only his eyes restless: the spirit was willing, the flesh weak? The tarted-up walker reminded her of a car her ex might still hanker for—not the professor, though, who drove a Smart Fortwo. His anti-Popemobile, he called it.

Ahead loomed the cathedral, appearing more monolithic than in the guidebook. A slight breeze riffled the hair on people's heads. "I don't want to hold you up." Hennigan's look was shy now, wary; a stranger's after all. Abruptly he stood. "Good of you to come—I've enjoyed the company." From someone else—the professor? her ex?—it would've sounded wheedling or resentful. But his face had a lambency, his words a sincerity that made her feel obliged to linger, and, wordlessly, to follow.

Beyond the cathedral a fresh throng gathered. As they approached, a hush fell. Swallows darted and dove. Through the crush Arlene spotted the cavern—the grotto at the centre of all the fuss—its shadows lit by flickering candles. "You're right. This *is* crazy. But here we are," Hennigan breathed, "the faithful gathered." Peering over a thicket of shoulders, she glimpsed a priest raising something—the communion host—and gazing down from a stony ledge, a blue-robed statue of Christ's mother. *Que soy era Immaculada Conceptiou*, said a plaque entwined with roses—the bush that had supposedly sprung from rock, the guidebook said, where Bernadette saw the Virgin's apparition. "Not two or three, but eighteen times," marvelled Hennigan. "Imagine."

A carillon muted the priest's intonations, intonations about Christ's body and blood, that fixation on flesh. Flames danced palely. Pilgrims groped and kissed the cavern's blackened walls. Drifting incense recalled the scent of wisteria in the rain—the way Paris smelled when she and her ex had visited it, not long before Em was conceived. A mature, vivacious blonde in a sheer red dress pressed toward them, thalidomide flippers dangling from her filmy little sleeves. Sunlight bounced from the gold cross swinging from a chain around her neck. "Same age as my wife, a child of the sixties—like yourself?" Hennigan nudged her. "How's that for the power of presumption?" He insisted that she call him Michael.

She glanced down at her toe; by now it was rubbed raw, all but numb. When she looked up again, she'd lost sight of him. Then there he was, closer to the river's edge, lowering himself sedately to a bench conspicuously vacant. She could have pretended not to see him, could have taken the chance to detach herself and escape. But he waved, tapping the seat beside him.

Perspiring and thirsty she sat, worrying her skirt's limp linen over her knees, dying to take off her sandal. But an awkward propriety prevented her. The strange, unsettling fragrance—incense—insinuated itself again; less the scent of wisteria than of carnations, or the disinfectant sprayed against fleas in animal labs?

Silently they watched an obese woman trying to raise herself from a wheelchair as a man cheered her on; it was as if the woman had all of eternity to rise and walk. "'Love isn't impatient or unkind.'" Hennigan's smile was wan.

"It'd be hell—" She caught herself, not quite in time.

"Being a cripple?" He drew in the walker to let a couple pass; they held hands, riding by on their motorized scooters.

"What God's brought together may no one put asunder." A line you could have fun with. She couldn't help its sarcastic lilt.

He cleared his throat repeatedly, part of his condition? "If you've had enough it's understandable." He produced a leaflet. Mass times, she glimpsed with amusement and alarm. Yet she stayed put, out of politeness, regret? Summoning things she'd seen on TV about MS—a new therapy in Italy—she let the clanging of bells hold her there.

Brushing dust from his pants, he arose, leaning less heavily on the aid. His face was creased yet handsome, unlike the professor's, whose receding hairline, hopeful mullet, and sharp eyes gave him a greedy look. Compared to his sloping ones, Hennigan's shoulders were ropy, his polo shirt a mauvy pink that neither prof nor ex would've been caught dead in. Carefully he unfolded a map picturing the bone-white basilica set against an impossible blue. A perfect stranger still, though already they'd spent much of the day together, if you could consider togetherness to be moving among the faceless devout—the *devote*, as people called their religious relatives in obituaries back home. Devoted to hopeless hope, addicted was more like it. But who didn't hope for something?

Her blister had crusted over. But a fresh irritation chafed her, dismay—disgust—at herself for not moving off on her own.

"If you could have one thing, Arlene, what would it be?" Amid the bells' pealing his question lit like a fly. Old women trudged past bearing candles, the type reserved for power outages. For no good reason she pictured Em alone in the dark with her iPod.

"To be in Font-de-Gaume—Fahdegome?—seeing the caves there, the prehistoric art. Short of visiting Lascaux, which they've closed. I'm sorry. Look, I'm keeping you—really—from your mission." That word stuffed with corporate purpose: crusades, high-minded and bloodily self-serving, and at their heart, a deadly self-righteousness. Worse than the absence of any god, as far as she could see, was human messiness, the failure of any system to temper it.

"Not a bit. You're not keeping me from anything. The trip certainly doesn't end here." He spoke brusquely but his look was open-ended.

The only explanation for behaviour, the professor said, was behaviour itself.

As they re-joined the throng, Saint Bernadette's name came up again. The sickly miller's daughter who'd seen the Virgin Mother repeatedly. Girl drinks from spring bursting from rock, gets cured of crippling asthma: he related it like a movie plot, laughing.

"Like blood from a stone, and smoke from a fire?" She was thinking of artists tens of thousands of years ago drawing pictures of animals using burnt and bloodied sticks.

A girl Em's age stalking past on metal crutches brought her back. The woman next to her—her mother?—was praying aloud: *Walk, ye sinners, walk; for whosoever shall walk in my light will be saved.* Arlene imagined the professor groaning. Yet in her mind a chorus sang, voices like Em's, off-key, and the sound fanned a strange heat through her. The sun was merciless, yet she felt a need to hoard something of it—beyond its fierceness, some vestige of pride? Because a charge of pilgrims was sweeping them toward a wall, its mossy stones fitted with water taps. Hennigan moved with a mute grace, the walker skimming the cobbles.

Joining a queue, he produced a tiny flask from his pack. Disgusted with herself, she dug fruitlessly through her purse—any bottle would do. She watched people stoop to drink, some nursing from the spigots like infants, others cupping palms, careful not to spill a drop. Youths filled wineskins, an elderly couple two large pop bottles. As if surrounded by desert, Hennigan bent and splashed his face and the crown of his head, slapped water on wrists and forearms, and all she could think of was bacteria: germs and all the world's tiny, lethal hazards. He seemed careful not to drink.

Miracle water—Miracle Whip? The same idea. "Liberation therapy" was the "miracle" procedure MS-sufferers underwent, thanks to some Italian, to clear arteries to the brain. The jugular? Going for the jugular was what her ex once accused her of doing, Em just a toddler the first time he disappeared.

"You don't wanna leave sicker than you came," a voice singled itself out. It was the brochure-waving lady from the bus. Next in line, trapped there, Arlene felt her scouring squint. Ridiculously, she held out her palm. The water's softness was refreshing, refreshingly ordinary, cooling her wrist. She thought of Em burning up with a fever. Behind her the woman was complaining. The tour company hadn't yet found another bus; their delay was being extended.

Around her, people were weeping, some even fainting, out of what she supposed was some strange gratitude. Hennigan eyed her intently, as if trying to extract something from her, some secret trouble? Because troubles encircled them, they were everywhere, no one immune from the ones surrounding them. The brochure woman, at least, had moved on. Undoing her sandal, Arlene picked dried blood from her tiny wound. Muffled prayers rose around her, so much vapour. She felt at once ashamed and lucky, and more than a little pathetic. If there was a god and s/he or it had a plan, why bother working on your own plans, wanting things that mightn't be included in it?

The world turned and would keep turning; nothing stopped—and certainly not her companion, wheeling off. Now was the moment. She could catch up or make a complete break, offer an excuse facing him later on the bus. Instead, something made her re-join the queue, even dart ahead apologizing to someone poised to drink. She couldn't have explained what, or why. The world didn't stop; neither did impulses.

Twisting the handle she let water pool in her hand, its dankness rising like the funk of empty streets at dawn—the streets around the station in Toulouse, sidewalks steeped in piss and the wafting scent of flowers.

Head and shoulders knees and toes, she imagined Em, tiny Em, singing. The parts of the child's body built into a song. She brought her palm to her mouth. The water's flatness piqued regret even as she tasted it. Flesh of her flesh, blood of her blood; Em had grown up faster than the mind or heart could grasp—the way of every child?—as if childhood had never happened. At the back of her mind, Em teased: *WTF? Next you'll be going to church.*

Out of nowhere Hennigan—Michael—re-appeared. His paleness and bright shirt were his only distinguishing features in the blur; the sunlight's intensity altered everything. His patient smile undid her. It was too late, much too late, to thank him for his company, his *help*, and field what remained of the day amusing herself. By this time tomorrow with any luck she would be leaving the Dordogne, having freely admired paintings by people who had lived so long ago they might not have lived at all; in the end who knew for certain what was actual or authentic, or that anything was as you were led to understand it to be?

The caves at Font-de-Gaume seemed somehow less important when he suggested supper, his treat: an early one so they could be the first on the bus once it came.

As they climbed the crooked streets, her toe seemed all but healed. He asked if she was thirsty and they stopped to buy *l'eau avec gaz*. He barely blinked forking out ten Euros, though his hand quaked rather badly. Ignoring it, he spoke matter-of-factly, describing Nevers and Bernadette's incorrupt body on view. Lying inside its crystal casket, hands and face as rosy as if the little saint were sleeping. Her convent room smelled like lilies, a sweet, peppery scent, he said; his wife had been the one who'd wanted to go.

She tried and failed to imagine Em's response. "You've got your health," the prof had said after the divorce came through, laying some exams on her desk while she fussed over emails.

How smugly, how decently the suffering of another could be downplayed.

All the way uphill the cafés were closed till well into the evening. They found themselves once more, she and Hennigan, at the hotel, where a girl was persuaded to bring sandwiches. They had the dining room to themselves. While Arlene was peeling the cellophane from her supper, Michael slid his hand across the sticky tabletop and touched hers.

In the lobby the driver paced, lighting one cigarette off another. The replacement coach had yet to be dispatched but would surely arrive by midnight, he promised. Repeating this in English, Hennigan—Michael—said he needed to lie down.

In her mind's eye her daughter yawned, and it occurred to her, not for the first time, that at age sixteen Em knew exactly what it was to feel deluded, disappointed if not cheated by someone's weakness. The limits of someone's love, and not just her father's.

It made no sense to rent two rooms where one would do, simply to rest and freshen up. The best room available was three flights up—no elevator. The effort of climbing stairs sapped Hennigan's strength, she could tell, lugging the walker for him, which folded like a stroller. The room smelled of ancient cigarettes and coffee, its yellow walls, carpet, and corner sink each an expansion of grim. The dripping tap summoned Pavlov and his German shepherds salivating at the sight of a lab coat: food, the memory of white.

Michael limped without apology to the bed. Settling into the sole chair, Arlene quietly removed her sandals, for an uneasy silence had spread between them, a silence now murky, freighted. Slowly her companion drew up his legs, straightened each at the knee, and stretched out.

The unlikelihood, the impossibility of anything more than silence pressed in, enveloping the room's dinginess even as its shabby appointments—solid things—seemed to resist it. Shielding his eyes against the lamplight, lying there he looked for all the world like a phone recharging. She should've rinsed her foot—there was a single towel, threadbare but clean—and left him then. It would have been the opportune moment, the right thing to do. Instead, her need, her tiredness mirrored there, drew her to the bed, every nerve tweaked, giving in; negotiating its lumpiness, she aligned herself with the edge: the edge of a raft. She pictured Em likewise adrift, spooned together at home with her current boyfriend, their breath trapped under her hot pink duvet.

The Pavlovian had kissed her: a febrile peck stolen near the photocopier while no one was looking. Sex would follow the faculty club dinner, she felt gloomily certain. If dinner happened; *if* she wanted it to. Dodging gossip and its complications was the least of it. Something about the prof's acute smile, his greyish teeth, seemed distinctly off-putting now. The feeling teetered then grew, that she could live out her life and not have sex again: it was possible the way many, perhaps most things, are.

Hennigan's kiss was sobering when he turned to her. It was gentle, chaste, and disinterested, and closed the door on needs and neediness, his and hers. Dismissive or weary, maybe both, he patted her arm. His breath smelled of the lozenge he'd been sucking—a Fisherman's Friend, sour and cool—breath distinctly unlike the professor's, which, that once, had been faintly bacterial. Like a hungry animal's, she'd resisted thinking. As Hennigan began to snore, she recalled a paper the professor had wanted distributed—not that she'd mulled it over, its jargon elevating what was common sense into science: how circumstances took a back seat to responses that were automatic, unquestioning. What mattered was association. If you believed something, your imaginings and the reactions they drew made it so. But didn't all of us long for, expect, more?

Em's name hammered inside her; Em herself so tough and delicate, fragile yet intact. Contradiction was reality's test, someone had said, as wisdom was stupidity's. It was Em's assurances she needed, not a stranger's. Fastening her sandals, picking up her purse, she imagined the prehistoric paintings: silhouettes of mammoths, bison, and horses hunting or being hunted, preying on each another. Barbed horns no more real or more genuine than the impressions of pilgrims' lips on the walls of Bernadette's Grotto, the Grotto of Massabielle.

From the parking lot an engine rumbled, a low, grating throb. She was lucky to find a payphone in the lobby, a working one, a relic. It would be 2 or 3 A.M. at home, Em maybe asleep. The only answer to any prayer she could've mustered would be Em's dodgy hello. But as she punched the numbers and the operator's voice clicked in, a queue was forming outdoors.

The driver, obviously relieved, stepped in to make his announcement. Eyes bright with fatigue, passengers were pushing forward; luggage had been transferred, hatches were being bolted shut. Everything but her purse and the clothes she had on would be aboard. She imagined Em's disgust, predictable, deserved or not. *OMG, You're saying you got horned up and tried to fuck a cripple?*

Sometimes silence was the only defence a person had. She tucked away her credit card. "The guy with the walker, y'all know where he got to?" the brochure lady was calling. She pictured Em the day her dad had finally moved in with his new partner. She hurried up the three flights of stairs. She pictured Em in the bathtub, water everywhere: tiny breasts barely covered, her navel ring mimicking the one in the plug. *You're such a douche. Everything he says is true. Wish I could leave too. Wish I had that choice.*

Breathless, she found that the door gave effortlessly. Inside, the room's emptiness breathed back. There wasn't a wrinkle in the chintzy bedspread, or in either pillow. The walker hadn't left so much as a track in the yellowish carpet. It was as if Hennigan had never existed, not a sign of him left there at all—without a trace he was gone, as though he had never stopped or passed the afternoon with her, as if she had dreamed the river, the cavern, their skimpy, uninteresting meals.

There was no sign of him downstairs either, or in the queue board-ing the bus. Had he dozed off in the shadowy dining room, fallen or had some mishap in the loo? A man in a Tilley hat went in to check. The driver counted heads.

Hennigan was not to be found.

Taking her seat, she thought of Font-de-Gaume, of its cave and its dark, flat pictures, and once more, of lips grazing stone, imprints left in hopes of blessing: safekeeping from doom? "*Merci pour votre patience, mesdames et messieurs. En cinq minutes nous partirons,*" the driver's voice crackled from the speaker. Bouncing into his seat, he adjusted his mir-ror. The sea of grey-heads nodded, exhausted but happy, you could tell. The better part of their lives were behind these people, yet like tired schoolchildren they were excited, jubilant, to be on their way.

"Please, wait," she almost shouted. But as the gears engaged, the night's cooling darkness closed in, and Hennigan's absence absolved and filled her with a strange relief. It was unlikely anyway that he'd have appreciated the outlines of antlers and hoofs, the evidence of human hands and their ability to outwit beasts and doom—doom of any sort. Unlike her, he didn't need to see in order to believe in things, she told herself, settling in for the last leg of her journey, and soon enough, on to seeing Em.

SOLSTICE

HE'D NEVER SEEN A KID WITH WHITER SKIN, HE WAS PRETTY SURE. A sparkly stud in her cheek. Eyes blue as a baby doll's that never left his face, except while inspecting the van and when she was test-driving it—his idea, the test drive.

"How much will you take for it?" she said, climbing out. She had a man's-man sort of voice. A shiver to it, though, there in the frozen yard, too cold even for Dog to come out of his house. She was skin and bones, he guessed, if you could've seen under those baggy black clothes—that uniform kids wore these days, the type that'd come out of nowhere to wash your windshield. Get away from my vehicle! he'd yelled last time, hadn't been to the city since.

"Well?" Those eyes of hers lit into his.

He'd play her a bit, maybe, a smolt on a line so to speak. That chain hanging down below her hoodie—it was hitched to a wallet, he hoped. *First you look at the purse,* the song swam through his head, better than the *rum-pa-pum-pum* Eileen and her girlfriends had blaring from the house, the festering, oops, festive season upon them.

"How much you got?"

"I can give you fifteen hundred."

Funny, a little girl being that direct. But he liked it, wasn't going to take no. These shoppers you got off Kijiji, tire-kickers usually, make *you* bend over backwards, like *they* were doing you a favour taking whatever it was off your hands.

I'm looking for something I can live in, she'd emailed.

Then she's just the ticket, he'd emailed back.

A pinging jumped from under her heaped-on clothes; clothes that put him in mind of tarpaper, sugar shacks, outhouses and the like. A cellphone. He let out a big exhale, to let her know he didn't have all day. The wife wanted the van out of the yard yesterday, and just the *one* answer to his ad! A kid who looked like Ozzy Osbourne's illegitimate spawn, only starving. If he didn't get this deal on the road Eileen would be inviting her in for Ovaltine and a bath. Or maybe not. *She* was up to her armpits in "craft"—crap, he called it, in his head anyway. Her and her friends having a few sips, making lamps out of pickle jars and plastic holly. He'd drilled the holes in the bottoms, driven all the way to the mall to buy electrical cords, skinny ones, white not green.

"I'm sure you can amuse yourself in the garage." Eileen had given him strict orders to stay out, she and her hens wanting the house to themselves.

The kid turned the phone off. "Sorry. So. Like. Okay? Fifteen hundred?" Goth girl, Eileen's friends, especially Susie the soccer mom, would've called her. "You'll take cash?"

"Done!" He hadn't expected money up front. Yeah, that was a wallet at the end of the chain. The van barely worth the cost of the safety check, but he wasn't going to argue.

A wad of mostly fifties fresh from the bank is what she hauled out. When she licked her thumb to count them, there was a B. B. on her tongue. The things kids do for glamour, he thought. Thank your lucky stars, Earl, she ain't yours.

Somehow he owed her ten bucks, the last few bills being twenties.

"Wait here and I'll get your change."

Instead of doing like he said she followed him inside. Eileen and the girls quit laughing right in the middle of someone's "Imagine!" Something about some kid down in Halifax. "Oh my God," one of them went. That Susie what's-er-face, the one and her husband that got on that wife-swap show a few years back on the CBC?

"Staying with you and Donnie for the holidays, is she?"

"Hell no. Not in this life."

"Just a sec till I get your money," he told the kid. But before he could grab his wallet he heard Eileen asking her if she'd driven before, she didn't look old enough, blah blah blah. The two of them in the hallway, a host of tole-painted angels and Smurfs smiling down at them, and those flowers Eileen bought every year that smelled like diapers or burnt wires piddled on by the cat. Then everything went quiet; there was just the crackle of the fake log in the fireplace and the snip-snip of someone's pliers and cursing when one of the girls, maybe Susie, busted her light bulb pushing it into the jar.

"Have a really great holiday season," the kid said, taking his ten. It was like the clothes gobbled it up. So many layers you couldn't tell what she might or mightn't have underneath.

Having the sense to wait inside, frig Eileen, he watched through the sheers. Okay, let the bugger start, please, pleeease. Last thing he needed was a bunch of women saying he'd taken advantage of some poor kid. Thing started like a charm, though. The kid pulled out onto the road like she'd driven a truck her whole life. Any luck and it would get her back to where she'd come from—the city, he figured.

Being on the up and up, of course, he'd remembered to write her a receipt.

For being near the city the park was pretty sweet. It had woods and a pond with a trail around it—except for the pond it was a bit like the park behind their house in Calgary where she and her sister, and all the other kids on the cul-de-sac, had played. Cul-de-sac: it made you think of a twisted intestine. A land of beige. Barf, puke, vomit, was how she characterized the house colours. Taupe, olive, cappuccino, was her mum's take. Just the other day, texting, she'd set Mum straight. *Fine. You get the last word*, her mum had put. If Mum could've texted a sigh she would've. *PS, I'm sending your present*, she'd added, *since I won't be seeing you. It'll be in your bank account, okay?*

The park was bomb, actually. It was near a subdivision too, but one with smaller houses and hardly any beige. The best part was the parking lot: like, pretty much empty, just people walking dogs, a trash can with nothing but dogshit to show for it, now and then a Timmy's cup.

The van was red, so it hardly showed the rust. So things were pretty perfect—well, as perfect as they could be. The back seat was gone (she probably should've talked the guy down, but what the fuck). More room for her stuff, whatever hadn't been nailed down in the apartment.

One day when real people ruled the earth, landlords, fucking capitalists, would see how it felt: it sucked having no power.

It sucked having no electricity, too, but that was the only downside.

The pond hadn't frozen yet, so there was water, and the woods to piss in. It didn't matter, really, that the water stank like bog. She wasn't into hair-washing and that shit. It was cool being crusty. An added layer of warmth, she kidded herself.

But the best thing about this place? The very best thing? No pigs. Not a single cop had come nosing around—not once in the five nights she'd camped here. So she could concentrate on making the van a home. "She's got room to burn," the old dude had said. Earl, Earl Joudrey, was the name on the receipt he'd shoved at her. Poor old loser, surrounded by those Martha Stewart whackjobs, that super-Martha-douche he had for a partner. Even if he probably deserved it. Mum had a sister who lived up around there somewhere. She'd met her just once, that was enough.

Did you call your aunt? Mum was always texting. Aunt Susie had two kids, and yeah, like, when she'd first moved east she'd gone there one weekend. They'd treated her like a freak. One kid wanted her to be his human goalie net, shooting pucks in the basement; the other watched her the whole time like she was going to hide the Lego up her rectum.

You could go there for Christmas. They'd like to see you.

Right. No fucking way.

What a beast, the van. The best present ever, thanks Mum. What a ride—not that she was going anywhere. On garbage day, up the road in the subdivision, they put out some sick stuff. A chrome chair. Some wood she made shelves out of, for her books and what clothes she didn't keep on.

In the middle of the dash she displayed her bobble-headed Jesus, and over the windows, posters from shows out west, bands from her "formative years," as Mum called them—and still tons of room left over for her own shit. The drawings she did of buildings that, once the rich scum that lived in them got kicked out, and the glass smashed out of the windows, would become things of beauty, things to value.

You need to find a job, Mum was always texting.

It made her think how it wasn't what you did but where you lived, your home maybe as much as your clothes that defined you. Gave you your identity.

Since she had time, and since it was the holidays—five days to Christmas, the festering season like that Earl dude said—she cut down a tree with her Swiss Army knife. Just thick enough to stick in the middle of the cable spool a jogger helped her wrestle aboard. An excellent table, it took up more space than was maybe ideal, with the shelves and the air mattress moved in. But what the fuck.

The subdivision people had a thing for decorating the trees in their yards with red, gold, blue, and silver balls. When it got dark she went up there and pinched some. A little big for her tree, but WTF. She picked twigs with dried-up red berries and arranged them around her dashboard Jesus. Right in the spirit, folks like Earl and his lame-ass wife would've said. The spirit being an instant downer.

It was crazy, and it sucked having to ask, but she couldn't help it.

Can you come out? she texted Mum.

Faster than she'd have thought, Mum texted back.

Oh Shannon, honey. You know your father hates airports this time of year.

He's not my father, she pinged right back. *I want you to see my place*, she started to type, against all better judgment. She could hear it already:

What's wrong with a nice warm apartment? Roommates? Working, or going to school? But Mum's ping butted in.

We'll send you a ticket.

Landlords sucked. Roommates sucked. Working sucked. School sucked.

U no I hate flying, she thumbed. *U no it like totally brings on my panic attax.*

There was silence for a while, the screen as dim as the parking lot before the floodlights came on. And then another text:

Why don't you phone Susie? She and Don and the kids would love to have you. They've got that nice place, I saw it on TV.

So now it was about property, it always came down to that—private property, the hierarchy of ownership, and people who just wanted to rub it in. All the same, she felt tingly-eyed and crampy, like she had a twist in her gut. The van, sweet as it was, a nod to some kind of economic imperialism if not colonialism, and for sure a threat to the environment IF she drove it. The problem was, owning your own place and not having anyone to answer to freed you up to share your luck, your good fortune, your karma.

There was this girl she'd met at a show, a girl with awesome ink, like, all over her; in the bathroom she'd pulled off her clothes to show her. Tomorrow night was the solstice, she remembered: a decent time to invite this girl over. They could do a bonfire, listen for coyotes.

Hey, come & chk out my place, she texted, and sent the bus number and directions. She didn't offer to pick her up. The truth was, much as she'd wanted no fixed address, a home free of the hassles of renting, the van had barely made it back to the city, eating a whole tank of gas getting here. Plus, it seemed like a bad idea to give up the parking spot.

The friend didn't text back; maybe her phone had died or something?

᷄ ᷄
᷄

She clapped her hands together. Two pairs of mitts, long johns, two hoodies, a jacket, and jeans barely kept out the cold. It was a drag how metal was a conductor, which she'd learned, like, in grade two. But she could handle the cold, and to warm up she walked past the subdivision to the grocery store, paid for granola bars and veggie dogs with Earl's ten-dollar bill. There was a bank machine, and she took some money out, left from the chunk Mum had sent. The good thing about bank machines was they gave out twenties, so you didn't look like a spoiled rich-bitch consumer pig buying a chocolate bar (the thing with fifties that sucked).

It was cold but she could handle it. It was light she missed, light that would've made things better—fuck the festive season, light was all anyone with half a brain wanted—the only good thing about all the fuss, the commercialism, the consumerism, the churchy crap with the kid in a manger and the we-three-wise-ass-kings: it was all just people looking for light.

On the way home she scored just the thing: some solar-powered lights, which she swiped off someone's lawn. They were shaped like snowflakes as big as your ass, and looked pretty sweet stuck in the gravel around the van. How *did* the sun morph into twinkly reds-greens-blues, in that sequence? Some things you didn't want to know, because right now some poor loser in China was likely eating rat-shit soup just so the western world could rot in peace-love-and-joy.

The big-as-your-ass snowflakes sparkled and flashed against the black woods, even with the floodlights making everything a weak, grungy yellow. She stuck the grocery bag under the tree for snow, the tree with its ginormous balls, and thought of taking a picture so Mum could see, see that it was mostly possible to live without selling your soul.

She checked for messages. Nothing. No *R u ok?* No *Hope ur nt alone.* No *Hope ur wrm.*

It was probably best that Mum hadn't come. She ate two veggie dogs from the package; they'd have been nicer hot.

"I wish you weren't so far away," Mum would've said if she'd been here. "I wish you'd get a job, get a place, get a—"

"Life?" she'd have finished for her. "I have a life."

If Mum were here she'd just be looking her over to see if she still had tits or if her hair was still brown or green or blue, like the last time they'd seen each other.

She wolfed down three granola bars.

Happy shortest day of the year, she texted her mother.

There was a ping, very faint, because the phone needed charging. No worries, with the adapter she could plug it in to the cigarette lighter; that was the quality of buying vintage.

The message was from Mum. *I've been looking into flights. If you still want me to come. Christmas n all.*

It's OK, she texted back. *I'm peaced out. Gotta bounce.* The last bit got eaten, the phone dying.

To keep from draining the van's battery, she stuck the key in, kicked the gas pedal, pushed it to the floor, turned the key, turned it, held it, just like Earl had said.

There was a funny little pause, just like someone under the hood trying to choose: will I stay or won't I? Before she could imagine an answer there was a *CHCHCHCRRRRRKKKK!!!* Like a million glass jars being stomped on all at once, so sudden and sharp the jolt jumped from the wheel through her fingers, and the Econoline jerked forwards. There was a bobbling, bouncing sound as balls rolled under the seat, and a sour-ass stink like paperwhites, those flowers that looked so pretty but smelled bad, those flowers in Earl Joudrey's hallway. The reek filled the van, and maybe some smoke, and she got out.

She got out, *fuck*, and stood there watching the snowflakes blink and glow blue. Sick, they really were, and blue as the world—as the pond and the parking lot and even the cul-de-sac in Calgary, if Mum and her dick husband had the hearts to wrap their heads around things, around *her*—like, the all-of-it seen from the fucking space shuttle or something.

The snowflakes lit wisps of smoke twisting up from the van's hood. *She's fried, dear, fried.* In her head that creepy old dude's voice— the guy she'd bought it off—oozed and slimed the dark, or tried to.

But the blue drowned it out, spreading and deepening before her eyes, the woods and sky popping with it. It was beautiful, all right. Even if it was cold out. At least she had matches. And there were sticks around, lots of sticks, from the dogs that walked and crapped here. No problem at all gathering up enough. Not a Tim's cup to be seen, though—there never was when one might be useful—and no paper besides her posters, drawings, and books.

She had to dig under a few layers to find it, but there it was—sweet—crammed into her pocket along with a Needs receipt for chips.

She lit a match, held it up to the little blue slip—the one with Earl Joudrey's name, and hers: *Received, $1500, in good faith.* For a full second the flame lit a halo around her hands, a nice warm glow, a blast of light, just before the sticks caught.

The sticks went up, no problem. They made an awesome bonfire. Mum and Susie and her crappy kids and Earl Joudrey and that fem with all the ink would've shit themselves. Really. You could have seen it from a plane, brighter than the flash of the world's biggest, tallest cell tower. Even Mum's dickwad husband would've noticed.

It burned so brightly, looking up, she could just barely, barely, make out the stars.

CROTCH
ROCKETS

T HE LAST, THE VERY LAST HE'D SEEN OF ROZ MCILWEEN—THE LAST she'd been within spitting distance of him—was her sliding off the back of his 750 Kow. Twenty-six years and three months ago, to be exact—before there was digital anything, before anyone had even mentioned "the information highway." Barely a blip in his memory, Roz, when her email popped up. She'd stumbled across his website, she wrote. *Figgered it had to be u, who else would be hawking bike parts on eBay?*

This was just the warm-up. She was coming back east for a conference, yes, a conference, in the university town just a couple hundred miles down the road from Torporville, as she called their hometown. Would he like to meet up? Not "hook up," as they said online. It wasn't so much her coming out of the woodwork as the thought of Roz,

Roz McIlween, doing a conference that hit like a dart. Poor old Rannie, he gave himself a shake, feeling like some soused old dude standing in front of the board's bull's eye at the tavern.

I'll pick u up there, he typed, after nursing a couple of cups of tea. He needed that long to think about it. The screen glared back from the dining room table as Ma settled in for her show, a *CSI* rerun. "Who're you writing now?" she wanted to know, peering up from her chair in the front room. Now he had the business up and running, she'd taken an interest in the computer, instead of being on his back to find a better spot for it.

"No one—" He took a long, last swallow. "Roz. You remember Roz?" Who he might well have got sucked into marrying, all those years back, when he was an idjit—a kid holding down a shit-boring job three thousand miles away in a place he hated. When life was like Niagara Falls all the same: a rush, and no shortage of girls, him just not knowing it.

"Oh. Her. The little one from out Brook Street way."

"The little one," he snorted, dribbling tea, wiping his chin on his sleeve. "That's right." Meek and mild little Roz, who'd always known exactly what she wanted. Good for her, they said, still said, around town. Ma too, now that he thought of it:

"I always liked that girl."

Ma'd never known the half of it; Roz had been a piece of work. All these years later he sure remembered, remembered this and the hope chest she'd had shipped out west once she had her own place. Her granny's Royal Doulton figurines set on top of it, and the time she'd lit into him for setting down his beer glass there.

The drinking Roz had tolerated, not his cigarettes though, stinking up the apartment—their apartment, after a month or two of him camping out on her sofa, when he'd gone out there for *her.* Then he'd got the job. Then the old man had died and home he'd come for the funeral—just for that—but seeing Ma so all alone, he'd stayed. Pretty simple, really. Only logical, like quitting smoking, which he'd done. By then, though, they were fighting all the time, him and Roz. Roz, for all her plump-girl good nature, was the type who measured and broke spaghetti so each piece was the same. Once she'd winged a beer can at him for setting his helmet beside her Balloon Lady, or was it Marie Antoinette?

"The type who'd make you a fine wife, Rannie Jessome," Ma had called Roz back in the day—though she hadn't objected to his staying home, her Rannie; and after a year or two his going back to Alberta fell off the tachometer, as he liked to think of it. "I can hardly leave *you*, can I?" he said, careful, always careful, not to sound resentful or lay blame.

Though, yes, Roz McIlween would've made a very fine wife, he knew when he ran into friends of hers who hadn't left—one or two of them, full of stories: Roz, Roz, this-n-that. How she'd married, got her nursing degree, and was making money hand over fist like everyone else out there, house to die for, nice car, blah blah blah. All of it flashed back at him like the cursor, black against white in the dimness made jumpy by Ma's TV. But it hadn't been so bad helping out Ma around the house—a fair shake—in exchange for sharing her pension cheques. "A fellow gets by," he'd say when asked. Who knows how things would've gone if he'd returned to McMurray?

Roz's reply boomeranged back: *Fantastic!!!!!!!!!!* Oh yes, and he'd heard about her divorce too, though none of its gory details, from her friend who worked at the No Frills. Quite the lard-arse, that one, would kill the shocks on a 1650, climbing on back. God forbid Roz had let herself go too—but it seemed a little off to ask for a photo. *Great*, he tapped back quickly, because some customers—would-be customers—had also emailed, one wanting a fairing for a Gold Wing, another a crankshaft for an antique Indian: nothing he had in the basement, that's for damn sure. *Out of stock*, he typed back queasily, as it fully hit him—the dart's target square in the middle of his gut: Roz wanted to see him.

"Rannie? Where you off to?" Ma's voice drifted after him when he stole downstairs. He needed a drink. *Frig*, he breathed, *can't a fellow have a bit of space?* Under its single swaying bulb the basement came alive. If anywhere was home, if there was anyplace he loved, this was it: his man cave—his father's rusty tools piled on the cement floor, heaps of bike parts arranged according to their function and not necessarily by model or make. Filling half a wall was the hulk of a hog he'd bought off a guy in the Devil's Pets, a gang two towns over. The goddamn thing had never run. Next to it was the bike he'd driven back from Alberta, the blue Kawasaki he'd been raiding for parts, propped on its kickstand, a picked carcass. Enough to make him weep, the mildew on its seat was like mould sprouting on bread. The tank had been dulled by spilt gas, its paint the lifeless shade of the ocean on days when he wondered, truly, why the fuck he'd come back.

Happily adrift in this paradise, this basement oasis, was Ma's new washer-dryer combo, like two shiny icebergs. They needed good appliances if he was doing the laundry. It was hard enough doing business without her demands: "Did you remember my nightie? My housecoat? Now don't be washing with hot!" You'll be in hot water, washing your own damn clothes, he'd think, then beat himself up for it, trying to fill orders. One from South Dakota once, a guy seeking parts for an ancient BSA chopper. He'd scoured the internet then given up. *A chopper, is that a kind of plane?* some cyber-bimbo had emailed back. If it couldn't be scalped from the Harley or the Kow or the heaps on the floor, it didn't exist.

Taking a healthy swig of rum—Lamb's 100 proof, the old man's favourite—he wondered what Roz would think of his business plan. Probably not much. Overhead, Ma tapped her cane—code: two taps, get me more tea; three, come turn off the tube, wouldja?—meaning she wanted to be helped upstairs to bed. Grabbing a grease rag, he mopped his brow. Its smell was half medicinal, and it too reminded him of the old man, who'd done a stint fixing cars before biting it. So—he took a deep breath: inhaled fossil fuel, imagined it cooking between layers of rock, prehistoric compost, a heavenly black ooze—Roz was coming, and he'd see her, yes, okay, he would, if he had nothing better to do and nothing came up—an appointment to cab Ma to, or a swim at the Point, or a ride on the 350 he kept outside: a crotch rocket, but all the speed you needed to get to the No Frills and back. He could always ask that one what her friend Roz was like these days, dig around on Facebook, at least find out what size she was. Not exactly fat, she hadn't exactly been a toothpick either.

A nurse, though, a nurse would take care of herself, right? Not let herself go the way women this age seemed to—strange, really, that she'd never come back. People from here always did, at least for the summers; sometimes in the last stages of cancer, just to prove they could. How long ya been home? they asked, like asking how long since you'd passed your driver's test, or the pearly gates. Anyway. This conference or whatever the hell she was coming for didn't happen for a week; plenty of time to back out.

A night or two later, not long after Ma went to bed, the phone rang. He expected it to be the criminal, the little ball of hate who ran the salvage yard a few streets over—one of the only businesses left in town, besides the funeral home and grocery store. A guy who'd cut out your eyes before letting anything go cheap. Watching the highways for crashes, he dealt more in car parts, his shop an automotive catacomb. If being a vulture was what it took to be successful, I'll stick to working online, thanks very much, Rannie regularly told himself; once the hog and Kow were picked clean, he'd retire?

"Is it you, Rannie?" Her voice caught him off guard. It was deeper, throatier, than he remembered, and a lot more patient. Its effect was like wiping out while cornering. She could've been just next door. Picturing a person with that kind of voice throwing things made it hard to speak.

"Well, well, if it isn't the lone stranger." He let his eyes cruise the ceiling, hoping Ma didn't hear. "Got your email," he said helplessly.

"Listen—if you'd—" A whirring on the line made Roz speak up; she sounded clear and direct but the opposite of pushy, and maybe too patient: "Rannie. If you'd rather not meet—"

"No—God no." He was sweating now, the rag out of reach, draped over a wrench. "Look, I'd be...Ma would be pissed, I mean, offended if—"

"It's just, well, I'll need somewhere to stay over—a place to lay my head." That same old teasing, smart-as-fuck way of speaking. But practical, Roz was nothing if not practical. The closest motel was thirty miles away, and doubtful her lard-arsed friend could put her up, that one's place crawling with kids and their crackhead friends.

The very thought made his Adam's apple bob like a toilet-tank's float. His heart chugged. "L-like I said, Ma would be real hurt if you... if you didn't—

"So," he asked in a rush, "what's this conference, anyway?"

Something to do with mentally challenged kids, he heard. She spoke as if talking to one right now, as if she were in a gym full of crusty-eyed teenagers with poked-out tongues. He pictured them mobbing her with hugs, her hugging them back. From the stairwell his tools blinked at him, freshly polished chrome. Then her voice, just as shiny. "So. How's business?"

The next evening didn't she call again: "Rannie?" No letting this damned visit drift to the bottom of his speed gauge, not for a second. "If you'd rather I didn't come…." Her voice was cheery but testy as the ones on *Coronation Street*, Ma's other favourite show.

"I'm looking forward to it," something made him mumble, when every ounce of him, chokingly silent, demanded, Why, after so long? From the dining room window he glimpsed the Newfie ferry gliding up the harbour in the dark, a boxy swan headed for open sea.

Ma hobbled from the kitchen with a peanut butter sandwich on a piece of paper towel: "That's her? That's Roz? Ask her what she'll eat."

"Food, Ma," he said, hanging up. "She'll eat food." As if feeding the woman was his worry.

"What's your biggest ambition in life?" She'd asked him this stupid question—this very question—in a *Jeopardy* voice, way back in high school, near the end of grade twelve. A voice like Alex Trebek's, poised and sharp—arrow-sharp, forget darts—straight to the stomach. They'd taken his bike into the woods, the first he'd ever owned. An orange 200 CC Yamaha with a classic dirt bike's forks. It was just after Easter break, with patches of snow and ruts in the mud, brooks and runoff splashing up—the back of Roz's jeans and her baby blue jacket were fanned with wet, though she didn't seem to mind. Sitting stick-straight and slim—oh yeah, but hardly skinny, he remembered now, with a little shock—she'd resembled a bug in her borrowed helmet. Her arms tightening around him, sailing over each bump. Abandoned farms back there, nothing left of them but small fields and apple trees. On a patch of dead grass they'd laid down together, nobody around, no one to see but the squirrels yammering in the spruces, a fallen-down fence, and the blue of a lake through the branches. Their hair was the same length then, his sandy-brown and hers a lot darker. Opposites attract, she'd said around his lips suction-cupped to hers. Her skin under her bra was winter-white when he managed, clumsily, to get it out of the way. "I really *really* like you," she'd said, closing her hand around him—as if saying this made doing it permissible. Talk about killing the moment, words that made him want to zip up and kick-start the engine. Of course he hadn't. He'd spread his jean jacket under her. Neither of them felt the cold, though when they stood the thaw had soaked through the denim. It felt like wearing a wet diaper on his back.

But he'd had this fantasy, about bringing her home for supper (Roz at the dining room table, Ma serving up corned beef and cabbage, and the old man draining his mustard-jar glass of Lamb's), till something had spooked him. What if they got lost, riding in circles in the woods? What if they ran out of gas? What—he'd climb a tree and watch while bears picked Roz's bones? And they had got lost, sort of, stumbling across an old foundation with daffodils pushing through the matted grass, an orchard hung with old man's beard, that greenish stuff like hair. Between there and finding the trail, he'd decided it wasn't so bad, her "really" liking him. A lot easier, less demanding, than if she'd said "love."

The rest of that year and into the next he'd eaten mainly at her house, though her younger brothers never quit pestering for rides on the bike. Around the same time, the year after high school, the arsehole who ended up buying the salvage yard got the hots for her and started sniffing around, before getting busted and doing time for joyriding. By the time the loser got out of Springhill, the McIlweens had packed up and gone out west.

"Son of a gun," said Ma when Roz and her family moved, just like that, lock, stock, and barrel, as she put it. "Not one of them stayed?"

"What do you want to *do* with your life?" Roz had asked when they finally broke up.

"Go to Sturgis," was all he could think of saying. Ride a big fat hog down through the Dakotas to the world's biggest motorcycle rally—and let life take care of the rest.

"Sturgis—isn't that where they've got the presidents carved in a mountain?" These were Roz's parting words as she shinnied off the Kow. Yanking off her helmet, she'd swung it at his shoulder, bashed him good enough to leave a bruise. Anyways, he hadn't made it to Sturgis and probably wouldn't—not now, up to his crotch in bike parts and laundry and a year's supply of Chef Boyardee bought with Ma's money.

It was nobody's fault—except maybe Ma's, for being what Dr. Phil might call "an enabler."

After that second phone call, not a peep—like the past was a self-cleaning oven, the kind Ma coveted though their cooking was easily master-cheffed by the microwave. Roz was having second thoughts, deciding not to come? Her silence felt like a reprieve, either the sweet, shaky calm before an apocalypse or he was being let off the hook? Suits me, he resolved, despite breaking into a sweat thinking either way, and meantime, that nut-bag Goldwing owner emailing six ways to Sunday wanting a head gasket. *Buy a new fucking bike*, he typed then quickly hit delete, replying instead, *Ask a dealer*. Did the whole world have him at their beck and call, working magic to bag whatever their heart's desire? A voice, the sane, sensible one in his head—like Roz's—interceded: Don't be unprofessional, it said.

To loosen the knot in his stomach, on a whim he took the 350 on a spin to the criminal's, thinking buddy might have a line on cheap Goldwing parts. The salvage yard sprawled between two vacant lots, each bordered by houses with plywood tacked over the windows and the hulks of dead cars outside. One thing he hadn't told Roz was that he'd come by bike to pick her up, if he went at all. Hefting the little Honda onto its kickstand set his heart pounding: his forty-eight-year-old heart, he reminded himself, rubbing his chest almost tenderly. The criminal's truck had what looked to be a van loaded on back, the vehicle crushed like a milk carton. Part of a lime-green Suzuki lay on the ground beside it. A donorcycle.

"Can't help ya," said the jerk, dug in behind the counter—extra large bag of Doritos and a Pepsi on the go, though the guy was scrawny as a ferret, a skull tattooed on his neck; was it the drugs? Didn't even look up from his video game, asking out of the blue, of all things: "Ever hear from that one out west? Bet you wish you were still doin' her."

The day before Roz was supposed to fly in—attend her conference and meet him later—Ma buggered up the computer, somehow pulling the plug while trying to vacuum. He just about lost it; didn't she know it had to be shut down properly or risk losing data? Was she planning to fork out the cash for a new hard drive? It wasn't how he normally spoke to his mother. On each trip for groceries at least one old bat asking after her would praise him for sticking around. "Least I can do," he'd say, humbled. "After all, who was it changed my diapers?"

With the screen gone momentarily blank the walls felt closer; the September sunlight caught their yellowish tinge, ancient evidence of the old man's smoking. "Holy crow," Ma flicked a dust cloth from where she sat, dabbing at the recliner's arms. "What'll your friend think? Rannie, it's not too late to get a rag, is it, and give those walls a wipe?"

Oh here we go, Ma milking the occasion to set him to work. The one bad thing about women, he thought: their fussing over things only they found important. "What time's she coming, anyway?" Ma huffed, reaching towards the mantelpiece, swatting a picture in its dusty frame: Rannie in his younger years. He pretended not to hear, rooting under some newspapers for a bucket.

After twenty minutes' scrubbing, his applying some real elbow grease, the yellowish stains hadn't budged. "Land sakes, Rannie—it wouldn't take any time to give 'er a quick coat of paint, would it?" Like the Second Coming, this visit, and as likely to happen now as the entire McIlween clan migrating back here—yes, she was milking it for all its worth. But keeping busy helped ease his mind and dutifully he dug out some paint from downstairs. The right shade, it took some chiselling to free the lid from the can. Ma was right, though. It only took an hour to slap some on, once he got it properly stirred—and the results were an improvement. Wrapping the brush in an old Harley-Davidson T-shirt, he threw it behind the dryer.

By now it was evening, and no word from Roz—no phone call to confirm or cancel, and no emails except from the Goldwing geek, he saw with some relief. But Ma was unusually edgy, jittery even.

"Make it an early night, Rannie—you'll need a good start. Your friend," she stopped to gargle back her thyroid pill, "where will we put her? Oh, she can sleep with me, I suppose. Still haven't a clue what in God's earth we'll feed her. I don't suppose she likes the Boyardee?"

"Listen, Ma—I know you're...I know you like company—" he said pointedly, though it wasn't entirely true. He lacked the heart to tell her what was beginning to look obvious. That Roz had forgotten or made other plans, having better things to do than see him—them—which in effect would be ripping the lids off dead old worm-cans. Poor Ma didn't have a whole lot to look forward to. He was searching for ways to let her down gently when the email pinged.

C u as planned, can't wait. I'll be ready, it said.

He tossed and turned the night away, then missed the alarm, almost oversleeping. The drive would take a few hours, and he meant to arrive in plenty of time. Still, taking Ma's sewing scissors to the bathroom, he trimmed a bit off his sideburns and more than he should have off the sides of his receding hairline.

The 350 ran like a hornet on the highway, zipping along light as air; even with a headwind he might've been flying.

The town was one he knew vaguely, its prim, well-kept houses and storefronts a far cry from Torporville's; people from high school had gone there to university. He had a good idea of where to find her, outside a gymnasium. Vinyl banners strung above the roadway advertised a "jamboree." Remembering too late how she liked flowers, he waited for a good half hour, smiling at the female students parading by. The sight of their tanned legs and sandalled feet helped calm his nerves. And then, suddenly, there she was.

"Mister! Rannie, it's you—it's really you, you made it!" Flying towards him, even compared to the many young things, she was all and more than he could have hoped for or expected. Her face was smiling and full, the flush in her cheeks too high and uneven to be makeup. She reached out a manicured hand and stroked his arm, then, moving close—

close enough to give a whiff of her warm, soapy smell—kissed his cheek, a quick, friendly peck. "I could hardly come all this way and not see you. Even if it's short." And she gushed a little, no, a lot, about how good he was, how sweet, to drop everything and come all this way— and on a weekday!—to see her. "You're too nice to say no, is that it?"

It took a second to realize she was teasing.

She looked a bit confused when she saw the bike, grinning. "Oh well—some things don't change. That's a good thing, isn't it? Good to see you. No, I mean, really."

His hands trembling, he managed—just—to strap her carry-on bag to the back.

Time had been kinder to her than he'd imagined, given her divorce and all. The years had added substance, Ma would say, Roz's arms fleshier but still supple, shown off by her sleeveless purple top. Threaded with grey, her hair was still long and thick, clipped to the back of her head in a twist that made him think of a palm tree. When she lifted a stray lock from her neck he glimpsed her bra, a deep pink—not a detail Ma would appreciate or approve of; Ma, who took pains in summer's sleeveless state to hide any trace of a strap, even one with Kleenex tucked under it. He was wholly aware of this as Roz straddled the seat behind him, also of her pressing lightly against him, fastening the spare helmet. The electric start worked first crack. Thank Christ the engine's burble made it difficult if not impossible to talk, especially once they hit the highway.

"That guy's still around?" she yelled in his ear, passing the criminal in his truck when at last they reached the nasty turn into Torporville. "What a vulture," he thought he heard.

Ma was upstairs in the bathroom when they arrived, in time for supper. The first thing he did was turn down the TV. That morning he'd cleared off a chair and moved his computer to the front room. Making an extra space wasn't a problem.

"Well, well," said Ma, hobbling in, beaming. "Look who it is." She'd nuked some chicken wings, and served them with macaroni salad—a type he didn't recognize—explaining proudly, "I took a taxi, dear, to get it. Not every day we have a nice little guest, is it Rannie?"

The dining room was sweltering, not a hint of a breeze coming through the harbour-facing window—unusually warm, wasn't it, this late in September, they all agreed. "Is the West this hot?" Ma wanted to know, clearing plates.

Limping back in with the teapot—its glued-together lid recalling an ancient mishap—she set her favourite cup and saucer in front of Roz. It was a loud sort of purply shade—the colour of Thrills, or, he couldn't help thinking as Ma might, if you mixed Roz's blouse and bra in the wash and the dyes bled. "My granny gave me it when I was twelve. Her way of saying, Behave yourself! I had three sisters, mind—who the hell knows why me? Anyways—when I turned sixteen I met Rannie's dad, I suppose he corrupted me!" And she laughed, a loud rattling laugh he hadn't heard in a while.

Roz turned the cup by its handle, admiring it. *For a Good Girl* was painted on one side in gold letters. "Now, I'll bet you deserved it, Mrs. Jessome."

"'Mrs. Jessome,'" Ma snorted, giving him her look, "don't be calling me that. To you, dear, it's Minah." She narrowed her eyes. "If you don't mind me asking, what business have you got in mind wit' my son?" Her voice stayed sweet: "How's your ma keeping out there? Queer, they never come back. They must love it, your people."

Sweating, he got up and put on the tube—a show on PBS about scientists, anthropologists, studying a native tribe. At least we speak the same language, he told himself, the three of us, sort of. Slapping the table—"Lemme show you what I been up to"—he moved toward the basement door, waving at Roz to follow.

It was like descending into a mine, the darkness near complete even at midday since he'd painted over the windows, an effort to hinder thieves. He'd have liked to leave things that way, utterly dark, Roz stumbling into him before he put on the light. His heart was beating crazily. Thirty years ago, he'd have reached out and unclipped her hair, just to feel it brush his wrist.

"Well?" Her laugh was dusky and nervous. He yanked the chain and his den, as he liked to think of it, filled with light. She blinked at the old blue Kow leaning there, blinked with a vague recognition, as if seeing the ghost of a ghost.

"This calls for a drink, I'd say." His vocal cords felt rusty.

From the kitchen Ma yelled down, "Dessert, youse two—peaches and a bit of poison, how's that, what Rannie calls ice cream."

He'd uncapped the rum, and held it out. Roz took a careful sip, wiping her lips with her finger. The grey in her hair was silver under the bare bulb, the look in her eyes about as helpful as computer lingo as she tightened the clip in her hair. He thought of that day ages ago in the woods, how she'd picked a daffodil—of all the things to find in a place where nobody had lived for years and years, maybe a century—and poked it into his helmet. They'd meant to go back to that place but never had, having found one by the shore instead, secluded enough despite its constant litter of smashed beer bottles and tissues.

"You're dead a long time," Ma liked saying, sure, and, once, he'd taken it to heart. When finally they'd shared a bed, he and Roz had done it like rabbits, honestly, like there was no tomorrow.

"We should go somewhere." His voice was desperate. "Let's get out of here, take a drive." But Roz was already halfway up the stairs, calling to Ma: "Whatever you have. Sounds good."

He found the two of them parked in front of *Coronation Street*, Roz asking Ma, "But what are his *plans?*" Her bare legs looked dimpled where her white jean skirt crept up; she crossed and uncrossed them. She could've been a dish of blueberry grunt in those clothes; dumpling limbs and purple against a dollop of cream—good enough to eat. Her gaze locked on Ma's program, then veered to the front room window.

Pulled up to the opposite curb was that bruiser of a tow truck, the jackass driver himself sitting there, just sitting, talking into his phone.

Something, Rannie wasn't sure what, made him go to the door and give the guy the finger.

"Didja have enough, dear?" Ma was asking. "There's more peaches if you want. Rannie, Rannie dear? Be a pet and get your friend some more poison." And to Roz, "Your folks—your father, your mother—they don't miss the old place at *all?* Not with the whole crowd out there, I suppose."

To everyone's relief Roz and Ma went off to do the dishes. A chance for him to check his messages, while he breathed as if oxygen-deprived. An email from the Indian owner said he'd tracked down the part in Sacramento, thanks but no thanks, and a forward from the Hog Owners of America announced next summer's rally in Sturgis. For just a moment, the voices from the kitchen stopped—or he stopped hearing them—and he saw himself in a long line of bikes, tanks and engines coated with Dakota dust: a line grazing the horizon, an infantry of ants, and between his thighs the glossy black of the Harley downstairs, except alive and purring. Then the phone rang. When he got up to answer it—Ma and Roz were oblivious—he noticed that the criminal's truck was gone.

He didn't recognize the voice at first, a guy saying he had a crank-shaft off a Honda someone had totalled—a bad accident a while ago on the Trans-Canada. "Buddy died," the voice said, "but she's perfectly usable."

"It's you," he managed to say, a sourness in his throat—a feeling like he was breathing exhaust.

"Must have something goin' for you." The piece of shit laughed. "She's there, isn't she—the McIlween one? Lemme know if you're inter-ested. We could do a swap."

Ma picked that moment to barge into the front room, dishtowel over her shoulder, ankles thick as tree roots as she collapsed into her chair. At least she was alone. "So, Rannie," she sighed, and pointed the remote.

He found Roz where he didn't expect to, down in his hideout, where no one went unless invited. She seemed startled to see him, glancing up from her perch on the Harley—he had this terrible thought that under her weight the stand might buckle and the thing tip over, pinning her. She'd gotten heavy, was the truth of it. Why had it taken him this long to notice? Not that she resembled her friend at the grocery store. But still. He couldn't help thinking of the girls at the university, the flexing of their long, smooth legs, and how they texted as they walked—like some species that had developed the ability to make its way without ever looking up.

"Why on earth do you stay?" she said, in the same tone Ma used, telling him, "You can't take it with you, Rannie," after his dad died—"it" meaning things like houses and cars, and simple comforts, he guessed, like liquor. But he'd spun Ma's words to mean the place itself, Torporville, which amounted to things put off, left undone, till it was too late, and all the false starts—the unfinished attempts and in some cases the attempts never begun—simply piled up and plugged the shaft that made up a person's life. After a point, why anticipate more?

Licking his thumb, he gave the bike's tank a rub, as if with care the shine might come up, to hell with rubbing compound. "I think you'd best get off," he said as gently as he knew how. He leaned forward so the front of his jeans just brushed her knee. For a second, only a second, he wanted to ask about her ex-husband—whoever he'd been—just to fill the hole between then and now: years as regular as spaces between bikes in a revving, rumbling column, drivers gazing at the dusty vista.

He was tired, tired of her, tired of her visit. Maybe she sensed it, putting out her hand not to push him away or pull him close but to keep him where he was. Her fingers touching his shoulder felt warm but not friendly, and sure not inviting—not the way, earlier, he might have wished. A limp disappointment took hold of him all the same.

"You're a good guy, Rannie Jessome. Good to the bone." Her voice was tinged with irritation and something else: regret? "Sure, I thought, maybe—well, I hoped. Who knows what could happen, after all this time? Stranger things have…I mean, people hook up—or they don't."

"Yeah. Yeah, that's it," he said, as the feeling—a grating, floundering one—moved from him, moved quickly, leaving him safe, washed up but oddly satisfied, content. In his mind a stream of rear-view mirrors flashed slices of helmets, leathers, and tanks with custom-painted flames. He could almost hear throttling, a Triumph's roar. She looked at him, curious, expecting more? He hadn't lived this long with Ma not to know that a lot of things were better left unsaid. But she slid her arm around him and pressed in close to graze his cheek with hers—his sideys still prickled from their date with Ma's scissors.

"You always were such a nice girl." It was all he could think of to say, glad of the dimness because his face was burning—as if he'd come down with some kind of bug. That anxious, he was, that keen to be rid of her. Some chirping came from her pocket: a squirrel trapped there? Her phone.

"Who *is* this?" Even in the cruddy light her look showed annoyance. "Not a chance," she was saying. "No, I don't want to meet you for a beer, or a Tim's. Look, I don't care how you got my number. I don't care if you're buying."

He wanted to grab it from her, and yell into it: She doesn't mean it, man—that friend of hers, down at the No Frills? She told me Roz is here to see you! No shit, man. He'd have called the criminal himself to be let off the hook. But, hanging up, she smiled as intently as when they were kids.

"Rannie—I've got another favour to ask. My friend, Char's, she's by the grocery—better yet, the bus depot? Could I get a lift? Look, it's been *so* sweet of you and your ma. But I need to get going. It's really true, I'm afraid—I'm sorry—but it's—well, you'd know more than anyone. Once you leave you can never, well, really come back home."

Ma hardly batted an eye watching them leave on the bike, though she waved from the window—that smug little wave he knew so well from all the other times she had won. Though he'd never be certain, she might've blown Roz a kiss as they buckled their helmets.

She was still up and waiting when he returned, just as the credits for *CSI* rolled.

"Such a good girl, Roz McIlween. I really don't know what's holding you here. But who am I to judge?" she said, shaking her head as she took the stairs one by one, under her own steam.

SAINT DELIA

THE TREES CROSSING THE ROAD SAY DON'T TALK, NOT IF YOU
know what's good for you, girl. Honest to God, Delee, put a sock
in it, they say, like Ma and Cal do every night—except the trees whisper,
swish swish, not like Ma and Cal yelling up from the couch, eating their
Crit'R Burger takeout: Nothing you say will bring him back, Delee. The
trees don't sound nothing like Ma and Cal, even when those two talk
nice and give me their fries though I'm supposed to be asleep.

The trees talk through my window, loud loud some nights. I talk
back but not with my mouth—put a sock in it—but with my eyes and
nose and the noise in my ears. Keep quiet, Delee, listen, they say. They
hold hands over the road like a bridge. Just listen: and that's the sound
when a car goes under, and another, and another. Once Cal yelled, Slow
down, you arseholes, which got Ma yelling too: Get out of that bed
one more time, Delee, and you'll catch it, s'help me! Then the TV went
loud and Chef Ramsay's yelling rattled the window.

Talk all you want—see if that changes things, Ma used to say even before Cal and critter burgers and *Kitchen Nightmares*, before I understood about For'mickmurry.

One day one of those cars will be Dad, I always said because the trees did.

Ha-ha, told you so! I'm yelling at Ma and Cal this night when the swish doesn't fade but comes into the yard, instead of chasing the cars down the hill past the blueberries and the lake and the other places we go, Ma and me and Cal. Since she came Cal goes everywhere we do.

But it don't matter, nothing matters, because here's Dad in the front room, and Cal doesn't even turn down the TV, the season finale, the cook-off between a pole dancer and some other lady which made Cal laugh her head off. Except, she stopped with Dad standing there. "How's my Delee?" is what he said and he hugged me then made me put on Cal's pink hoodie lying there. You could fit two of her in that, is all Ma said and then, "Well well well—things too cold for you in Deadmonton or For'mickmurry or wherever?" And no one said another thing except "Back to bed, Delee."

Dad went out and slept in his car. I know because the trees said and Cal's shoes were on the mat next morning—her mucky ones for work. When I went outside Dad was in the back seat with his boots off, smoking a cigarette. He said, "Hop in, honeybunch; you be the driver, okay?" And I said, "Is For'mickmurry a thousand miles away or what?"

"That's about it." And he laughed. "No, it's a bit further, actually. But you can still drive if you want." So he stayed in the back and I got in the front and he made road sounds while I turned and turned the wheel till Cal came out and got in her truck and took off.

"Fuckin' diesel dyke—who'd of guessed in a million fuckin' years?" Except he wasn't really talking to me, maybe to the tree with the rope and tire and the green Big 8 bottle Cal puts birdseeds in. Then he said, "Come on, girly-girl. This is gonna suck. But I didn't come here to eat toast, did I. First thing I thought of when that one phoned was you."

"Cal's truck eats gas." I figure he should know.

"Go get dressed. Guess I should be grateful. But since the flat-arsed bitch isn't here to help, you're coming too. "

I knew he meant Cal because her butt looks like a desk. This I know from school, which I hate. Ma says I can pick blueberries this year till it snows and never go back, but Cal says we'll see about that. My house my rules, Ma says.

"We're going somewhere special? It's two-for-one at the Crit'R Burger." Another thing Dad should know.

"Sure are. Can you tie your shoes, Delee? There's a girl. See, I knew you wouldn't forget. She taught you good, your ma." Then he laughs.

Inside, Ma is drinking cold Timmy's, putting on her flip-flops. Dad sees the cat. "Who let that fleabag in?" Ma is laughing till she looks at my sneakers and her face changes. "Don't you know, Delee, I frigging hate that purple." And Dad says, "Take it easy, Frances. Let's just go for a drive, okay? Delee, I need you to get in the car."

I don't want to at first because maybe he's taking us to For'mickmurry. Long car rides make me puke. A Sobeys bag with Ma's toothbrush and product and stuff from her top drawer is on the seat. The tires' spin sounds like blueberries being squished, the sound in the Quonset where Cal works, that looks like half a juice can. A bee flies in and buzzes, You don't have to do nothing you don't want to. When it flies out again, Dad remembers I have work because he pulls in by the field.

"Give your daughter a kiss, Frances. Let her know you'll see her soon. We'll catch you later, honeybunchofoats."

"Catch ya later," I say. But Ma doesn't turn around. Cal's hoodie is over her head and she makes the same sound as a Timmy's ice-cap coming through the straw. That's the last I see of her for a dog's age.

In the blueberry field are birds Cal taught me the names of: nuthatches, robins, juncos, chickadees, sparrows—I know them all, picking and picking. Going for the best berries, my fingers are Sidney Crosby and the bees are the Maple Leafs fighting for the puck. Nice deke, Delee!

a blue jay says. It reminds me to ask if they have birds in For'mickmurry and what kinds. Now there are more important things than what you can see, the bush says, and I'm God picking a gazillion blue apples in a heaven that goes forever. One basket, two baskets, three baskets, four baskets. The wind cracks up the sunshine—relief from the heat, Ma would say. I'm thirsty but the only drinks are in the shop, wine the owner gives people in cough medicine cups and water from the machine, which costs one loonie and one quarter. All I have is a loonie. And I need to fill the flat for the tractor. It looks like a blue baby quilt Ma found at Frenchy's that Cal made her put back.

"How many baskets?" the tractor boy says. "Count 'em, idjit." Sticks and stones will break my bones but names will never hurt me. Dad taught me to say this but I don't. I could ask for a quarter but would rather eat a cow-pie. The boy throws an empty flat on the grass then drives away. I'm so thirsty. But the hilltop and the woods are green as Kool-Aid so I drink them in with my spit and high up like this get to be a bird or an angel like the pins in the Pharmasave. Be a guardian for mental health, it says on the box. Cal got one for her and one for Ma to stick on their fleeces.

Ma got me my job. Better than Xbox, she said. Cal got her the job weighing U-pick berries and gluing on labels after Cal puts the wine in the bottles. It's like nature, Ma says, how it's all connected. "When are you gonna grow up, Delee?" she also says. "Nah, forget I said that. I like you as you are—you know that, don't you, curly girl?" Why does she call me that? My hair is straight as grass. She said it once at the lake, with just her and me and no Cal. Cal still had work; "Chicken fingers for supper?" she'd said, waving to us. Remembering makes me hungry. It's been a long time of dark and then sun sun sun since last night's fries, and no sandwich like Cal usually makes, Kraft single, ham, and lettuce with no mayo because mayo goes bad, Cal says. I would die for a mustard sandwich but no dice, as Cal also says. I do not want to ask her for a quarter either.

Berries squish between my giant fingers. The sun has crossed the lane where cars spit dust. The tractor boy says, "Why don't you knock off early, stupid? Who's gonna know? I won't tell nobody." He throws my second flat onto the back. "Gonna take yourself for a dip? I seen you, you and your crazy ma, down the lake. Gonna take it all off for me, Delee?" He has no shirt. When he drives away, his wing bones stick out. Berries bounce like hailstones. The shadows too are blue, eating the field the way waves eat the the ocean beach not the lake's. If he stays for a while maybe Dad will take me to the beach-beach?

"We'll see," he says and when I ask the other question, about birds, he says, "What do you think? Sure there are. I mean, there must be. Crows, for sure. I just never really looked, tell you the truth." You would think that he picked berries for as long as Ma and I have been alive, the way Dad talks sometimes. Cal must have to work all night because she doesn't come home. "She's missing Episode Two," I say but he shakes his head. "I'd feel for her, Delee, but she's a little hard to reach." For supper there's Crit'R Burger wings and fries. "Hit the hay now," he says, even though it's only early. "Back to work in the morning." He doesn't say where Ma is or how long she will be there, only that she's a case and that Cal doesn't help. "Boxy Lady," he calls her. He finds the cough medicine she and Ma keep under the sink and tries some but spits it out. "You'd have to be desperate to drink that. But who wouldn't be, eh Delee? Living in this place."

When he's sleep-dead on the couch I sneak outside and listen to the stars. They stutter when they talk, spitballs flying everywhere. That's what they look like against the black black sky, from where I'm laying. The grass is so tall car lights can't reach through. I keep staring up but get buzzy, then listen for closer things, spiders and crickets and the wind's sh-sh-sh and the hum that says back to school. Suffer, I could tell that tractor boy, but won't, though he deserves it. When fog hides the stars I wipe the damp on my shirt and go in.

Walking never hurt anybody, Dad says. What's a little rain? So I walk to work and again the next day and the day after that. By now the sun has come out, hot like the dryers at the Spin 'n' Go where Cal takes our clothes when the well dries up. Funny that the rain came when Ma left and Cal decided to stay away. Just goes to show how some things clump together, but not a cluster fuck like Dad says. Cal's truck is parked by the can, so I guess she hasn't gone far far away like Ma. While I'm picking she comes down the hill with Doritos for my lunch. It's a family-size bag so I really won't go hungry, and she gives me a toonie and says she's not out of the picture—pitcher, she says, so I picture her as a June bug floating in a jug of ice water at the Crit'R Burger when you eat in. For one second there's a sound like a blueberry being popped when she hugs me to her boobs. How can a square person be so soft? It's hot, too hot, and Cal smells like wet bark or maybe raccoon pee in the bushes but probably what I'm thinking is just sour, a smell like fall. But her bug eyes smile the same as when her favourite person makes Chef Ramsay say nice job, and I know Cal is not like Dad thinks. "Catch ya later," she says, not a question.

After the tractor boy takes my last flat I'm so flipping flipping thirsty I go all the way up to the machine with the toonie and buy water. The owner's dog, Bluebell, licks Doritos stuff off my hands. Her tongue feels like the lake bottom. "Git!" I say but don't really mean it. If I had a dog I'd name her Bluebell too. This Bluebell is brown like an Aero bar. She licks my bottle too. The sun spikes off of the juice can building and off of the shop roof, so so hot, and if Ma were here she'd say "How 'bout a dip, curly?"

"What's the matter, Delia—forget where you're at?" It's the tractor boy saying my name, my real name, like Cal used to at first. He rubs Bluebell's chin. "Goin' for a swim? Fuckin' school, right—only a couple days then the shit starts. Bunch of us headin' down, should be good. Gonna follow us?"

I don't say it—Suffer—because his voice not his talk is like Chef Ramsay's telling me, Too late. Got something to say, say it sooner. The tractor boy's talk is like Dad's talk: Nothing in this shithole changes. But the trees and the sun and even Bluebell say, Delee, just go cool off.

The lake is down a road that throws rocks under cars, which is why Dad won't go. Why put something that's mint through that? Bad enough the frigging salt in the air—jigging, I mean, jigging, he says, like I'm a big copycat. My sneakers scrape and my shirt feels like lettuce Ma would put in the sandwich she'd have made if Dad hadn't taken her away. But soon there's the path through the snake lilies and tea berries and poison ivy.

Out on the water the teenagers rock the wooden float, jumping off, climbing on, over and over. The girls have bellies like dolphins that do tricks on TV, boobs and birds covered with triangles, pink, orange, green—colours like Kool-Aid, which Cal says is pure sugar. The boys shake themselves like dogs do, flicking their wet hair. One could be the tractor boy but I'm not sure because they all look the same. Then he opens his mouth and yells and I can tell it's him. He's pointing and yelling, "Don't just stand there. Take it off. Come on. We seen your mom do it. You can do it too—we want to see you!" and he says my name-name.

I stand there in my sneakers and my shorts and shirt and after a while I take off my sneakers and let the lake touch my toes. It makes the rocks look gold and my feet yellow, as in *if it's yellow let it mellow if it's brown flush it down*. I keep my eyes on the place where the gold turns brown and the brown turns black as Pepsi. The lake's licking-lapping makes me picture Ma taking off all her clothes and diving into the lake's belly. The skin on her bum a bit like orange peel only pinky-yellow like grapefruit, which Cal says makes you gain weight, forget what magazines say.

"Come on, Delee! Do it for us. Show us, come on, show us!" the boy keeps yelling but then another boy pushes him off the float and a girl is standing up and she says, "Ohmygod. Don't be such dicks." Their voices are louder than the lake which says come in, come in, I like your green shorts, Delee, and that orange top: what colour can I turn them? Even louder it says how it will feel wrapping around me like the slippery-cool see-through scarf Dad brought back for Ma once.

The teenagers are wrestling now. They're skinny but shiny and wet like WWE wrestlers and they're throwing each other off the float and now the tractor boy is doing handstands, only his feet sticking up out of the water, and a girl screams Ohmygod an eel and another screams Ohmyfuck, a bloodsucker. "Fooled you, asshole!" the first girl says, and the tractor boy yells, "Your ass is grass and I'm gonna smoke it" and jumps up on the float and throws her off. And quietly the lake says it's okay, they don't see you anymore, Delee, so I walk into the lake, my shirt heavy like snow once I duck and duck again—like there are golden hands pulling on it, pulling me down underneath to where the mud is like Bluebell's tongue only a lot cooler.

No way hosay, I think too late—the same as with Suffer. The things I should have said. Too late. The boy follows me down the path. His feet make no sound but I know he's there. His fingers hurt, digging into my shoulder. There's the smell of snake berries—a blue smell but not sweet like blueberries, that have a shoe-polish taste, Cal says.

The boy's feet are white against the dirt and dead leaves—I keep my eyes fixed on them. Delia, he says, Show me, show me, he says, and I don't know what he means even though I can guess. The hand he steers with tries to push into my shorts—but they're cutting-tight and hard with wet, and a little red dragonfly comes and lands on his arm and sits there. I think it really is a darning needle, like Ma says, sewing up his mouth, because he doesn't speak. Now his hands are to himself. Keep your hands to yourself, the teacher says in school. The dragonfly flies off and the boy runs away but the drum inside me goes Ma, *Ma*.

Cal's truck is there—I see it even before I reach the Hidden Driveway sign up the hill. Dad's mint car isn't, though. Cal's inside making supper, putting juice on the table, saying to leave my wet stuff on the stoop after and she'll hang it out. Up in my room I put on the jammy pants and Frenchy's shirt we got before Dad came back and any of this happened. Rock Your World it says in sparkly letters. Downstairs I put the wet clothes outside. The underpants and shorts look like a fat hair-band inside an even fatter hair-band. Large and larger, Cal corrects me when I say it.

Her hands are purply-grey like mine, what happens when you work with berries. She drinks right from the medicine bottle and doesn't bother putting it under the sink again.

"I want Dad," I say but Cal is busy scraping hot Highliner onto plates, and there's a thing of mint-green coleslaw on the table. "A healthy alternative to Crit'R's," she says.

After we eat, Cal watches TV with the sound off and her eyes closed. It's a good chance for me to go out and listen to the grass, except it speaks in a voice like the tractor boy's. "How's she goin'?" it hums and hums, and when the sky turns pink to purple to grey the clouds then the stars are too weak to talk. "Where is For'mickmurry?" I asked them the first time Dad left. "Nowhere you want to be, little girl," Ma answered instead, calling me inside. "It's outwest," she said, the time she took off all her clothes and got water up her nose. Now I might just take it to Jesus, like Cal said to do once. Take 'er to Jaysus, Frances, which made her and Ma break out laughing. So taking a question or a problem to Jesus must be like putting it in a bag and hanging it on the doorknob so whoever's taking out the trash won't forget.

Lying under my puff—Hey, a puff! Ma and Cal both said, pulling it out of the Frenchy's bin—I think of them and Dad and the tractor boy and the eel and bloodsucker girls and Bluebell, and how each could be in a bag marked Donations sitting on the front lawn, Jesus pulling up in a truck and the tree branches waving hello, hello, and Jesus opening up the back and throwing them all in, and me lying up here waiting for the trees to say what next? Then where would I be?

I ask them, is Ma ever coming home?

Sticking her head in, Cal says G'night, Delee, and not to hold my breath.

♪
♪ ♪
♪

Dad comes back and it's Sunday, the day the berries are U-pick only. When I wake up I hear him talking to Cal and after a while he comes upstairs and says we're going to see Ma. "Is she at the beach?" I say, because I want to know, Are we ever going there?

"Don't you have any other sneakers?" he asks and says to wear a clean shirt and pants because it's turned fallish. This is news to me and I think how the teenagers will be mad if it's too cold to swim on their last day before school. "Suffer little teenagers and go jump in the lake wearing clothes," I say.

"What?" Dad goes. "Delee, you've been playing too many video games."

Cal has on new jeans and a fleece top with *BlueHillsBlueForYou* and three berries on a twig sewn on the front, and her little mental angel pinned on too. Her hair is combed so you can see the comb marks—does she ever think about using product like Ma does? Probably not. She doesn't mind having blue fingers. Ma dips hers in Javex to get the blue off.

"Is Ma in For'mickmurry?" I ask, just to be sure, because even though I'm so excited to see her I could almost pee myself, there's the car ride, and I know it must be long.

"No," Dad says and looks at Cal in the mirror. She lets me sit in front and takes the back seat, saying it'll give him time with me—to prepare, is what she says. Prepare—isn't that a word an apple could say, for instance, waiting to be peeled? Except I'm not a fan of apples, except in the turnovers at Mickey D's and Timmy's—places named after boys. Which reminds me, what is the tractor boy's name? Travis, that's what. Tra-vis, don't be a dick, the eel girl screamed.

Because I'm scared of throwing up, Cal passes me the bag from Ma's stuff—a pack of cards, peppermint patties, underpants, and the rest piled on her lap. "Wanna give me some advance warning, so I can pull over," says Dad. I know he's worried about the seat.

"Nice car," Cal says, but not like she really means it. Even riding in the front, I would feel less sick if we were going in Cal's truck. Then I wouldn't have this worry that we'll take a road not to Ma but outwest.

The city has a big bare hill in the middle and buildings taller than any trees. It's raining. Dad parks the car and we walk up to the hospital. The entrance is like a humongous inside-out basement, cement with plants growing, and people outside smoking cigarettes, hardly talking. The cars going by have more to say, but maybe that's just me. Cal has Ma's things in the Sobeys bag, which I'm happy to say I didn't need to use. She carries it the way the eel girl probably carries schoolbooks.

Inside the hospital is bright with walls the colour of that girl's swimsuit. Strangers smile at us. Dad gives them dirty looks and Cal tries to take my hand, but please, I'm not a baby, I'm twelve years old! In the elevator Dad punches the button that says 7. The door closes and when it opens the walls are purple. Down the hall a man in a yellow shirt sits at a desk behind a thick glass door, and there's Ma! She's looking at us, looking at me, as if she's been watching for us for a long, long time, and oh I hope she isn't too upset by that wall or seeing my shoes. When we get right up to the door the man in yellow buzzes it open. His arms are tattooed black and blue like someone has drawn all over them with a Sharpie, snakes and swords and stuff. I'm so busy looking I almost forget to hug Ma.

"Go on, Delee, give her a good one, you came all this way." Dad nudges me forward, standing back. It's Cal that hugs Ma first and Cal that Ma hugs back, it's Cal that Ma wants to see. When it's my turn Ma sniffs my hair and looks at my sneakers then hugs me too too long, because the man with snake arms is saying move away from the door. Dad's feet move like they're separate from his body, like they could step through glass and down the hall, out into the rain and into the car and step on the gas to go back to For'mickmurry. Like, if they could, they'd move faster than stars can blink.

Cal says "Why don't you give us a little tore, Fran." So Ma does, she takes us on a tour down another hall and around a corner, past a bunch of closed doors with people's names written on pieces of paper in red marker, past a room with a window and a sign that says Tranquility Room and another that says Family Room. We end up in front of two shiny metal doors that look like the kind on the back of trucks that pick up cases of wine from the can, bring bales of clothes to Frenchy's, and buns and fries to the Crit'R Burger, and so on. "You so don't want to get put in there," Ma says. She's holding the Sobeys bag but doesn't look inside.

Walking Ma to her room, waiting for a man in jeans who says he's a nurse and comes to unlock her door, Cal says it's time someone stepped up to the plate. I think about those white plastic plates burgers come on, with fancy edges to make them seem real. Dad puts up his hand, I think to fix Ma's sweater sliding off her, but then says he needs a smoke and Cal says me too.

"Coming, Delee?" they say.

But I won't leave Ma. I won't leave her by herself in here.

Ma turns to the wall on her hard little hospital bed. I lie beside her, my knees in hers, my arm around her stomach. It's like hugging Cal's bird feeder in the wind. How come I can't remember what it felt like being inside there? The trees would've known where I was, before Ma did—they talked before she had words? Once, crows built a nest over the road and even in a hurricane not one baby fell out. The good thing is there's a window. You can see treetops down below. We're two birds in a nest now—look, Ma. But she doesn't answer. There's just the feel of her stomach going tight-tight, holding something in, like her skin is a tight but still-stretchy shirt.

Listen, then. You'll hear them. Listen to us, Frances, I try again, in their soft, soft voice.

And she says, Get him to buy you new shoes.

Not for school! I think of her skin, her pinky-gold skin under the lake, and I think of the tractor boy putting leeches on people's backs—not ours, though.

For school, not for school. Whatever, Delee.

But I really don't think she's listening, not to the trees. Maybe she can't and never could hear them and never will be able to, what happens when you don't want to. When all you do is grow too big to.

So he's here now. You were right—he did come back, didn't he, she says.

Then I remember the dead grass in my sock, a little tiny piece from that last time listening to stars. I pull it out and hold it to my mouth, hold it like Beyoncé saying thank you, thank you very much.

This is Delia speaking. This is Delia, Ma, and because I am the only one here I guess you have to listen. I am not a tree but I am here and you can tell me everything. Everything. Because you're here, here I am, listening.

SHELTER

AN INFATUATION, THAT'S WHAT IT WAS—OBVIOUS NOW, BUT then? Not at all. Wait long enough and the past sneaks back— maybe while you're unpacking groceries or leaving the mall—in this case, during my weekly stint at doing good. I was serving coffee. A street-scarred hand reached for a cup. Thick, callused fingers. I could just imagine the condition of their feet as the line moved forward, a shuffle of misery.

Against what life dishes out I count myself lucky: driving here each Wednesday, locking my purse and down-filled coat in the staff room. My husband says, "But don't you find it depressing?" Well, yes. But it's the least a person can do—payback for being fortunate enough to have a home, a car, boots with treads.

Did I mention this was February? The cruellest in years. The men were complaining of booms waking them in the night. Gunshots? The weather girl on the flat screen was describing snowquakes: icy buildup cracking the city's bedrock. My husband didn't see why I couldn't miss a week or two to escape to Cuba; someplace, anyplace warm. Why we couldn't be snowbirds like others our age.

The client with the large, especially rugged hands, wrapped now around his Styrofoam cup, said, "Jesus, imagine." His wryness made me look in a way I usually avoid. His eyes—one slightly lazy, the other piercing—seemed oddly familiar. His gait, too, when he beetled back for his refill; one per client keeps things fair. Slight and balding, he seemed robust but stooped, owing maybe to rough physical work, shoulders hunched in his red checked jacket, head bent forward. The posture of a ghost? The shiftless but resolute way he moved, both agile and aimless, shook then broadsided me.

"Can you stay longer today?" Marnie, the counsellor, was asking, needing someone to help the nurse coming to do foot care—a volunteer to distribute donated socks and boots. A local rock star had started a footwear drive for those who slept here: the addicted, mentally ill, unemployed, and others desperately short on luck.

"Sure," I said, though all I wanted was to grab my things and dash to the car. A normal feeling post-shift, except more urgent than usual. Waiting for the nurse, I busied myself making more coffee, collecting used cups.

Slumped in their coats, men were glued to the weather channel. Along with being dry the shelter's non-smoking, but with a windchill of -35 who could enforce this? "What the fuck?" someone laughed at the looped item about snowquakes.

Rolling a cigarette, Peter sat transfixed—by now I could only think of him by name—the anchor-girl's voice tinny-bright above muted ones. "In Guatemala," I heard him say.

"Fuckin' Guatemala," spat the man beside him, grinding out a butt.

Offering a glimpse of the harbour, the Beacon's windows are greasy Plexiglas. Its walls are dented and dinged, their pale yellow grimy with nicotine and grief. A strip of blue sky beckoned, or the promise of snacks at the soup kitchen a few snowbanks away. When the nurse arrived most of the clients had vanished, the familiar one included. "Looks like you're not needed after all," Marnie said with a shrug. "Good for next week?"

My husband watched me unzip my boots in our sun porch. "You okay?"
"Why wouldn't I be?" I said.

I need to tell you, I must explain: it was that and *no* more—an infatuation. Though it's easy to look at something thirty years on and dismiss it as such. A girl in a hippie dress, I'd been, barefooted but not, thank God, pregnant. I remember as if it happened last summer, my gazing over the bay from a homemade bed snugged up to a hatch for unloading fish. The building was an old fish store—a warehouse—built on the rocks.

This is how I remember it. The dry dust of July coated everything, yellow dirt from the road behind us thrown up by the odd passing half-ton truck. Few cars went by. Flies buzzed in whatever windows had glass. A skim of sawdust everywhere added to the dirt, the smells of creosote and fresh-cut lumber rising from the workshop below, and the scorched stink of an ancient hotplate complicating whatever stuffiness the stiff sea breezes couldn't drive out. At summer's height it grew stifling—one long, glowing Saturday is how I recall days parcelled out yet sprawling too, shaped by nature: fishnets of sunlight cast up into the rafters by the waves whose sound I awoke and drifted off to at night.

If it sounds romantic but gamy, it was. I don't even want to think about the outhouse sunken into the hill across the road, barely enough soil there for digging the hole—easier to pee in a jar tipped into the sea. *The ocean'll take 'er away, boys.*

CAROL BRUNEAU

Bodily functions, never romantic, are best wiped from all memory.

If I were so inclined I could make up a story of that summer—its predictable arc jazzed with court and spark, to coin that Joni Mitchell title. But, levelled by time, the truth of it stays as flat as a prairie; building a berm or two to add some grade would be false and unnatural, purely sentimental. Being sentimental would mean shaping the story as I would've back then, shaping it as the biology student I was—into birth, life, death—if I'd had the patience, the interest, to put any of it on paper. To create drama out of all that takes devotion, and devotion—real devotion—requires love.

Making a love story here would be more than a bit precious. It's easy to say what fed my infatuation. You were a good ten years older than me. "I can't believe myself—a twenty year old!" you said—derisively, I refused to see. Berating yourself for walking into some kind of trap—*if* I had been old enough, sensible enough to listen.

"Your face would stop a clock," you said once. That was the extent of the compliments you paid me, referring to the first time we met. It was at a folk festival; I was driving through the field in my friend's car. She and I were smoking weed and suddenly found ourselves in the ditch, a parade of feet streaming past the windows, which at the time seemed cosmically funny. You were the first thing I saw when I jumped out—you and your bus. You were lighting a joint in the driver's seat, this ancient blue school bus parked there with Beautiful B. C. plates as exotic as you. Your black coffee eyes, your waist-length ponytail and cheekbones that looked Central American said you weren't from around here—no way. But I had seen the bus before—who wouldn't have noticed it parked down the hill from my parents' street? I'd taken to walking by just to see it, a sort of landmark amidst the bungalows, the sign of someone's hippie relative returned from the west? The wild west of communes and non-aboriginals living in teepees. The west that in stories I soon would hear featured these and handwritten vegetarian cookbooks, bulk grains, lost love, and serious addictions—some vague, restless grief on your part, I see now.

Without a second thought I hopped aboard. You had a Maharishi smile, a Colonel Saunders southern gentlemanliness about you, the way you held out the roach: "Toke?" My friend had gone off to party with

110

whoever had helped free her car. Still giddy from watching all those feet, I was alone with you—the bus had just the one seat and I stayed standing. Inhaling felt ordinary, boring even—predictable to share the butt end of a joint when we might've shared conversation or our names, for starters (the thought of which makes me laugh a little now). Then some partiers crowded on and I went to find my friend. The whole thing lasted maybe three minutes.

I honestly can't remember how or where we met again, only that when we're very young stuff happens fast. Soon there was sex. You were never possessive, urging me to have it with other people too though I was—I am—stubbornly monogamous. There's not much to say, except that the romance included flannel sheets in need of washing and lentils that stayed bullet-hard despite boiling for hours on a hotplate.

There was the sea's lapping, yes, and the flap of wings: gulls' wings and crows'.

You smelled of sawdust and clean sweat. Your broad-shouldered, deeply tanned body was compact and wiry. You had a perfect six-pack and were an eyeful working shirtless when I'd sneak downstairs from playing house above—which I did for a time that summer—to the squealing buzz of power tools. Early on I may have expressed some interest in using them, not entirely a ploy. You showed me how. I appreciated the band saw's swift, neat cut but balked, always, at the table saw's teeth. Table saws still make my head swim with images of women in boxes being sawn in two, magician-style.

The chests you crafted to sell to tourists were twee pirate ones with rope handles and curved lids—small trunks for dreamy sea voyages. The scent of their sanded pine dispelled staleness. Because there was staleness, the kind after much drinking: red-labelled Olands and cheap Hungarian wine—sex on Saturday was how we said its name—and, in your case, rum and Coke; I remember your fondness for rum and Coke. Also there was weed, hash, and coke scored from boats hovering just offshore and snorted from a jagged scrap of mirror.

Yours was a world as dangerous, remote, and as alluring as British Columbia seemed back then. You were a migratory bird choosing between up- and downdrafts, the riskier the better—if choice figures, figured, into anything.

A studious girl with a sometimes interest in cell division, with you I easily play-acted at being what I wasn't, charmed—then—by those who flew without safety nets, without much in the way of wings, even: people unconcerned with survival. It was fun to flirt with what the safety of my grounding frowned on, having, for instance, a mom just edgy enough to buy health food, and the fact that your mom lived near mine.

"He's yours now, you take care of him," yours said once—imagine! You might have been from some previous generation: why would I want to catch up with it? But you had that allure, and it wasn't as if you were mean, or unkind. "Patient" would describe your judgmental hippie non-judgment, call it pacifism or apathy, a zen detachment or simple disinterest; if not for racing hormones, you were a brotherly older companion. I followed you places my friends wouldn't have.

I revisit this now, recalling it. The way some people note the taste of a certain coffee, you described doing heroin: the rush, nothing like it. Any tracks on your arms had healed over, veins roping over carpenter's muscles—you had those powerful arms. Not once did you utter the L-word, your honesty pressed to the limits by my presence—your forbearance. You'd done too many acid trips to lie like that, you said; had fallen too hard and too deeply for someone once, then crashed, left to burn by a woman who'd driven your bus.

Traces of her popped up: yellowed notes, a stray glass bead here, a wooden one there, and in the excess width of the Guatemalan hammock you strung between two studs. A curled snapshot—too faded to reveal more than her smile and Janis Joplin hair—showed the two of you partying behind the wheel.

Did I ever imagine or expect that I would see you again, that it would be in a shelter for the homeless?

Without a trace of bitterness I remember a wilted sprig of wild laurel on the floorboard by your bed—blooms like tiny pink umbrellas—left by someone, someone else, not you, not me. Apart from your endless supply of lentils you had no interest in flora, other than in trees for timber; boards that with nails and screws could be fashioned into something to breach waves, brave the seven seas. I remember the buckets of salt water and the fires you built under them, steaming planks into bowed shapes: pipe dreams of sailing the oceans in a homemade ship.

My first and only clue something had tilted, had changed, was that dried twig, its spiralling leaves and flowers. The commonest of plants in the woods of my childhood, so ordinary as to go unremarked—who would be so dull, so limited in their choices as to pick it? The same pink, those miniscule blossoms were, as my dress, which I'd sewn myself. Ragged inner seams, gathered waist, long skirt: a polygamist's idea of sexy, my husband would joke if he knew, picturing women in modest cotton with long, straight hair—their appearance screaming of some sociopathic male greed.

The romance outlasted summer but barely, in the end simply petering out. One day I caught the Acadian Lines bus back home. But I remember the last time I saw you, a few months later. You were in the city on an errand, the city where I'd gone back to school. I had a backpack loaded down with cellular biology texts. You were driving through this busy intersection in your truck—the school bus by now turned into scrap— and we spotted each other at what felt like the very same moment. You pulled over and, before I could run away, got out. The sky was grey, I remember; it was raining or, possibly, snowing; the first, wet snowfall of the year. A city bus stopped, releasing its passengers. Among them was a sandy-haired guy I recognized vaguely from third-year ecology class.

You had nothing to say, except to explain that *you'd* decided to stop seeing *me*. (When my friend with the car heard about this, she laughed, "I can't believe it.") You mentioned, offhand, somebody's name. I remember part of me wanting to curse you up and down and even take a swing with my backpack. But it was way too heavy and cumbersome and, anyway, you didn't give me the chance, jumping back into your truck and peeling off.

The guy from ecology must've seen me struggling, because he offered to help with my backpack. "Here," he said, and shouldered it all the way to class. This was the first time we'd actually spoken, and we ended up having coffee afterwards. "What were you so mad about?" he wondered and maybe, years later, he still does.

It's not something I've gone into, not even when he teases about how "shipwrecked" I looked that day—crushed, bereft, furious—that first time he really noticed me. Quite a first impression, I must say, to leave on a future husband: the sweet man, retired now, who eventually became mine.

You and I never spoke again; but once, your mother phoned.

"I don't expect to see him ever again," I said in a voice frigid enough to snap the line.

The following Wednesday I report as always to the Beacon, in time for coffee duty. There's an abundance, an embarrassment, of cookies past their best-before date, a truckload gone stale after sitting for days on some whited-out stretch of highway between here and New Brunswick. Coconut and chocolate chip—your favourites. For all the millet you stockpiled, you had a wicked sweet tooth, I do recall.

But when the coffee's fixed and the snack set out on plastic trays, when the men line up you're not among them. I scan the room—let my eyes linger by the TV, where I'd expected, hoped, to see you. You see, I planned how I would approach you; I'd decided it was better to own up, to speak as if we might have something to say. In meeting your direct, knowing eye, I aimed to see the past melt and slip by—a chunk of shore ice loosed from rocky moorings, set adrift to dissolve and disappear.

I was mostly just curious to see if you remembered me.

But as coffee time begins and ends there's no sign of you, only the others I've come to know by sight if not by name—the ones who, week in and week out, rely on this place. Then Marnie comes up, helping herself to a cookie, and says, "Missing someone?"

I can only shake my head and smile at the nurse coming in early, hauling a box full of gauze and antiseptic. And I hear her say, "That was too bad, the other night—that guy they found by the bus stop? Got him to hospital anyways—at least he passed in a comfy bed."

From under hoodies, faces glance up. "Peter?" Marnie nods, then shakes her head. "Sad, for sure. Yeah. Oh well."

A life lost is never less than that—nor is the severing of a tie great or small, even when it's an infatuation left unfed, with nothing to fuel the work that love demands.

The end of the life in question lent my own a circularity, I guess. Putting on my coat at the end of shift I felt older, definitely more winter-weary than when I'd first learned the art of brewing coffee in two-hundred-cup batches, but liberated somehow, too. Liberated from the shadow side of life's open-endedness, the skittish urge to flirt with exactly the nothingness that cuts us, all of us, adrift.

The sun shines and the snow falls on everybody indiscriminately, I liked to believe—whether we squirm towards or away from either, seeking comfort: love, you could call it. The kind that asks nothing in return might seem the safest—but might also be the most dangerous, knowing, as it does, no limits.

As I dug for my keys, men dozed before the TV. Through a Plexiglas blur, ice pellets showered the pavement outside and dulled the harbour's desolate blue. Someone handed me an empty coffee cup, muttered thanks with no hope of getting a refill.

"Sarah. Can we count on you again next time?" Marnie called from behind the desk's bulletproof glass, and without much hesitation, "Of course," I said.

"What's up?" my husband asks. "What's wrong?"

"With—? Should there be?" Before I can hang up my coat and slough off my boots he's standing close, inspecting me as if something has happened, not to someone else but to me.

"Have a hug, Sarah. You can't get enough of that place, can you."

I put my hand to his warm, wrinkled cheek, the sandy beard now white. "I'm fine. Really. It's all good." Which it is, which it must be, in

the diminished way of marching age which knows the shelf-life infatu-
ations have, even before they begin. Safe, always safe, they do not ask
more than any one of us wants or is able to give.

the VAGABOND LOVER

THE BEDSIDE CLUTTER WOULD EASILY CROWD OUT ANY BOOK—
Styrofoam cups, straws in paper sleeves, tiny boxes of hospital
Kleenex jockeying for space, these and the disconnected phone taking
more room than it deserves. It's not like she'll be calling anyone, with
the crispness of outdoors creeping in, creeping through—Dolly can
feel it penetrating the window that faces the sea. The ferry cutting a
path through sea smoke on its way to Newfoundland: this she pictures.
Hardly needs to see to do so, or to feel the hard frost pulling the last
leaves from the maples. *The world in solemn stillness lay.* A kind of carol
rings in both ears, ears not much good for hearing anymore but with
a new acuity, one all their own.

Her chest lifts and falls. The book's safe, that's something. Never
mind it's missing its cover—a mishap at a caregiver's hands. No longer

a grave concern, because its gilt lettering stays in her head. "My treasure," she tells the nurse, who swabs her lips. The tiny pink sponge on a stick she calls a mouth mop. The book a sort of Bible, pressed leaves and flowers crumble between the pages—dust—and a typed-out verse tucked there too. Cut from the *Herald, 1927* jotted in her hand, the same as the inscription: *To Dolly Cutler from Jimmy, Xmas 1935.* Penned so she wouldn't forget.

So much room to forget; and who knew all this would take so long?

Blind to the clock's face and the nurse's, her eyes distinguish only daylight from dark.

"What's the hour? What, only ten o'clock—not noon? Gad, is he on Cape Breton time, on pogey, the Reaper?"

More deaf than she'll ever be, the nurse squeezes her hand. "Hang on, darlin.' You're soon having a birthday—did I read that right?"

Her 107th: who in God's acre needs reminding? A ridiculous, ridiculous age.

"No fuss, do you hear me? I won't want any fuss." Being polite, she coughs up a laugh.

You can't take it with you, they say.

But like a treasure in an Egyptian's tomb, maybe the book will follow her? The cover, adrift somewhere, lost perhaps in a stack of magazines, is or was rust-coloured cloth. Graven in her mind are *Bliss Carman's Poems* and a laurel wreath in gold. "Our poet laureate," a voice prods through the brightness, enough to give her a charge.

Bliss's lines brim in her mind: ants. They crawl over the whiteness of walls past the ceiling. Wherever the room empties into is grey-green: the ocean?

The nurse's shout is tender: "Pain, Nana? Are you having pain?"

As ridiculous as living so long, being called 'Nana.'

Cold tea held to her lips. The fumbled straw.

"Allergies, darlin'? Ever been allergic to anything, hon?"

Her soul pulses. Words come from her throat: None, nothing, except to marriage. A flutter: numbness. The same feeling as in her fingers, the nerves hushed as if she's wearing furry gloves.

"I could've, might've, should've married him, I suppose."

He couldn't wait to give it to her, hot off the press, an utter surprise—the nicest gift anyone could've thought of. No ribbon, no wrapping besides the paper it was shipped in. He had it there at the station when she returned from one of her jaunts. Home from Halifax, Toronto, Quebec?

Never could sit still, could you Dolly? No grass grows under your feet.

She was twenty-nine, just turned. Come back to find everyone she knew married, on to their third, fourth, even fifth child.

"So what's it like up there in Ontario?" The first thing he said, greeting her.

"It's all right. You find nice people everywhere." Then she said how the sun had flattered the alders by the old shore and Little Pond when the train chugged in. "Gold, pure gold—even the cliff jutting out, the one like an animal's snout. I wish you could've seen it."

"Me too—I'd have liked that." Anyone else would've said she was cracked to notice. But Jimmy tucked her hand in his inside his coat pocket. His coat flapping open, no time to button it, hurrying from the office. Down Main to Legatto Street, past the washplant and the bakery at the first far-flung hoot of the whistle. He'd wanted to be sure and get there before anyone else could.

Soot on the snow, coal by the tracks—winter had come early that year. His footprints and hers made a tandem trail through the back gate and into her parents' yard. The narrow grey house crammed with kids, her brothers and sisters, was no place to take a fella. Nowhere you could expect a warm cup of tea or a handshake, not from Pa anyway. From Pa not even a "Who'd you say your father is?"

That Christmas Jimmy pulled a few strings and got her hired on at the British Canadian Cooperative—the Co'p as they called it—in the store adjoining the office. She waited on miners' wives out to blow their men's wages playing Santa to hordes of kids. An orange for every sock in town, notwithstanding lumps of coal—clinkers from the stoves more apt? Humbugs, jawbreakers, and china dolls, tiny tea sets, prams big enough to carry swaddled kittens: just some of the things she sold.

She endured the job by plotting her next move. Nearly a decade since she'd tried putting the place behind her, going off to art school. The first paved streets she'd ever seen were down in Halifax. The school some drafty rooms above an undertaker's, fresh coffins on the street below. During classes the sounds, sometimes, of mourners.

His people—Jimmy's—were from the next town over, where ships loaded coal. A place of wharves, houses with widows' walks and turrets, its roughness was more genteel than Lazytown's. No hungry miners burning things down. Pa and her older brothers worked above ground: she had this to her credit. Though it made no difference to Jimmy's widowed mother and sister who had little use for her, she could tell, when invited to tea. Watching the docks from their window, seeing the boats that would take you all over—to St-Pierre, St. John's, Quebec City, Boston, New York.

Jimmy had soft hazel eyes and a mildness, and clean hands if a little ink-stained, and fine, strong wrists—from pushing paper, her brothers teased. That day coming from the station, he'd set her suitcase down behind the garage where the boys' Model T awaited spring's potholes and Pa's model ships rode waves of tools. Jimmy held her hand to his cheek and leaned down to kiss her—had to lean quite far, she was that short. She liked the scrape of his clean-shaven jaw against her smooth one, the warmth of him and his smell—of India ink and, possibly, the oil that greased the hinges on the office safe.

"Aren't you going to ask me in?"

With all her heart she'd wanted to and would have. Wishing not just the once that the house could be empty—abandoned—but for the fire in the kitchen stove, another behind the parlour's grate. Tidy blue flames. Pa and her older brothers at work. Ma and the smaller ones off at some church social, its basement hall festooned that time of year with paper chains and snowflakes hung beside the belching furnace. But no such luck.

"Tomorrow, maybe. Or next week. Christmas Day for sure," she'd hedged. Afraid to say it wasn't him personally, afraid to say it was.

So they'd arranged to meet when he got off work. "We'll go for a bite, see a show?" Shivering in her velvet coat, she pictured them promenading up the wooden sidewalk, slush pushing between the boards. *Scrooge* in lights on the Strand's false front—a mockery of Dickens's *Christmas Carol*.

"I've got Pa—why pay to see that?" Movies made you fall asleep; why not read the book instead?

"Right—you can sleep any old time around here." And he laughed, mentioning a sign in the church foyer: *Pray till something happens*, it said.

Then she'd kissed him on the lips and, grabbing her suitcase, leaving him there behind the garage, hustled past her mother's frozen garden and in through the porch. The smell of finnan haddie and carbolic soap to greet her, and Ma's shy, desperate hugs.

"Who was it brought you, Dolly? Not the young fella from the Co'p? He served me once when the girl in dry goods couldn't. Came right out of the office, he did. Nice fella."

And Pa: "Oh it's you. What, the wind blew you here? Decided to come down to our level, did you. What fella?" Turning away when she might've kissed his cheek. When she'd have just as soon kissed his cranky arse.

Letters, she thinks of, lying here. Ones penned on creamy paper, and the kind typed one by one on a clean page. The doctor comes to speak to her. She's clear in her head, perfectly lucid. But whatever they've given her leaves her restless, worrying the sheet. Better to refuse their medicines, though the oxygen helps. Without it, the heaviness is an animal on her chest.

"There are no cats in here, are there?" She has always hated cats.

"No cats." The doctor pats her hand. "The hospital won't allow them."

Her voice pushes up from the heaviness, muffled perhaps. Words, rhymes? And he hears her; the doctor has no trouble that way.

"So you like poems?"

He's a youngster—his voice tidy like his touch and the way she imagines his gait. He presses a coldness to her bones through her johnny shirt—a jimmy shirt, why couldn't it be? All she consists of, bones and skin older than the church, the oldest building in town. The raw bones of a bluebird are what she pictures, or Ma's bony fingers miming a steeple: Open the doors, Dolly, and see all the people.

There, now: *whenever you're ready,* she hears. Her cue. "'Some quiet April evening, soft and strange,'" she begins.

♩ ♩ ♩

Two days before Christmas they were packed into that basement like sardines, half the town there for the recital. He was right beside her— her beau! A bowl of punch on the sweets table, not a bit of kick to it but oh well. People raising a toast glared when he started to cough not a minute into her first verse. He'd coached her, trading off lines over sips of iron brew in a booth at the Five & Ten, the book opened to the page. That night she didn't need it, not for such a short piece, and left it home out of harm's way. The paper chains rustled in the draft. A bad flu going around that year, so bad three of her brothers and two sisters had already missed a ton of school. She had to speak over his coughing:

> *"And my lonely spirit thrills*
> *To see the frosty asters like a smoke upon the hills.*
> *There is something in October sets the gypsy blood astir;*
> *We must rise and follow her,*

When from every hill of flame
She calls and calls each vagabond by name."

Her young man, not so young at all measured against the other bachelors, by then few and far between, beaming and applauding as she took a bow.

⌐
⌐ ⌐
⌐

"You have a tumor, remember. In your throat. When we did the scope, that's what we found." The doctor's voice is needlessly careful. The malignancy could just be coal from the cars shunting past while Jimmy kissed her that day, wet snow soaking their shoes. A misshapen darkness giving promise to light? She wants only sleep, enough of this living longer than anyone has a right to.

"Have you forgotten me?" she asks the blueness. "Are you on vacation, or what?" A translucence winks back, blueness through the windowpanes: "Pray till something happens."

"A gold nugget inside a black lump." This she says aloud to make the doctor feel better. A coldness echoes down the shafts of old flights of adventure, past escapes. *What, Dolly, is your secret?* The secret of making it to this tremendous age; some still ask. No husband to fuss about. How she laughed telling people this, relishing their reactions: envy, sober second thought, a grim delight.

Coal seams under the ocean are emptied out, tunnels quietly collapsing.

It's important that she tells somebody—in the interests of science?

"I didn't have to stay single. Once, you know, I had fellas beating down the door." Only a partial lie—there was a man who boxed, a couple of others during the war, and even a minister, who allowed his cat on the furniture. Too Presbyterian for her liking; and she never could abide felines, certainly not in the house.

"Be sure to tell the nurse,"—this man, the doctor, bends close, too close, his breath in her ear—"if you're having pain."

Yes, she could have, should have married Jimmy.

Where there's tea there's hope, says the plaque someone gave her one or another Christmas or birthday.

With any luck he'll have some waiting, a full pot and a plate of Ma's fat archies to go with it. His desk cleared and the safe locked for the night, a fire in the office's potbelly stove.

No grass grows under your feet. Never mind grass'll soon grow over them. The rest of that flu-ridden winter she'd stayed put, and that spring too, figuring out what to do with her life while helping Ma. The littlest not even four years old, hardly old enough to tend whatever baby or babies might come next. Working at the Co'p she made enough to keep her youngest siblings in candy. Six pairs of blue eyes staring up from across the counter, these didn't include her two older brothers'.

'How many of there *are* yuz?' Jimmy liked to tease. What made the job bearable was glimpsing him through the office door, busy at his figuring. Garters on his sleeves, a visor on his head, he looked more banker than clerk. And this didn't touch the Jimmy who sat beside her at the Five & Ten, reading Bliss out loud.

"Will you come out to the country some Sunday?" he invited her early in June. Two ways to get there: by train or having one of her brothers drive them. But if they gave themselves all day they could walk and be home by dark.

Ma packed ginger beer and molasses cookies to sustain them. Oh she'd brought him home by then, one Saturday while Pa was safely off on a toot, at one of his 'meetings' behind the machine shop. Between scrubbing the floor and rushing to get the Sunday pies in the oven, Ma made an extra place at the table, yelling to the boys to stoke the fire but not enough to burn supper.

"Pleased to meet you, pleased indeed," she said, picking dough from her sleeves, fighting her surprise at the bunch of lilacs Jimmy handed her. "Not for me?" The only men who brought flowers weren't men at all but boys, four and five year olds clutching fistfuls of dandelions.

"I believe he'd like your hand, wouldn't he?" Ma's voice was cagey, almost sly, when that Monday morning she was helping with the beds— so many sheets. Bundling them up, bringing them downstairs to be boiled on the stove for whitening.

"Why else, girl-dear, would he be so sweet?"

For two solid years before any of this he'd written to her faithfully. Words crawling over the British Canadian Co-operative Society letterhead on which he also copied out poems. Sent them weekly while she'd worked in Quebec designing neon signs—that bold new brightness you'd never dream of in a coal-mining town—and up in Toronto designing tombstones. In memory of. Here lies. No winged heads like the angels on Lazytown's scabby stones but stylized urns, wreaths, and crosses, plenty of crosses. What else could she do with her diploma? Scholarships had got her through school; her way of seeing was what some, most of all Ma, appreciated.

Not that Ma ever said so, she didn't have to: A gal's dead a long time, Dolly. Use your brains. Better yet, be a bird and fly out of here.

Answering Jimmy's letters—enclosing the odd verse from *The Toronto Star*—had seemed safe enough, from that distance. Romantic, even. But then the work dried up and that Christmas she'd come home.

"What," said Pa, "people aren't dying anymore?"

The Sunday they walked to the country started off drizzly and dull. Mist sprouted from the fields, hay as shy as fiddleheads unfurling along swamps. The coltsfoot by the ditches was gone to fluff but in the woods, starflowers and lady's slippers bloomed everywhere. She carried Ma's refreshments in a bag tied with string. When they reached the Point, well past noon, they found a good flat rock for everything.

A finer fat archie he had yet to taste, Jimmy said.

Wet beaded the spruce needles, clouds thick as work socks hanging over the flat-topped mountains on the far shore. The lakes as far as you could see were one big mirror shimmering grey to blue when the sky tried to clear. Still the dampness clung to their clothes and the air had a nip. He kept shivering and she regretted bringing ginger beer, wishing there'd been tea instead—not that he minded. "It's only cold staying still, Dolly." So they walked some more, past a spot he pointed out where they'd look for chanterelles come late August, to one where a hawthorn bloomed, a fragrant billowy white. Coughing into his sleeve, he said before she could that he'd never seen a bush so loaded or smelled air so alive with its scent.

It had gotten that way, one stealing the other's thoughts.

He put his hand over his mouth to cough; he'd had this stupid cold all winter, couldn't shake it. "It's not a cold," he said, "just a tickle." And he seemed fine, healthy enough, kissing her—all over her face, it felt like. Enough to make her blush, though she kissed him back of course—though if it had been summer and there'd been people around she'd have told him to stop, she'd have had to.

As it was, it was cold, beyond chilly and damp as they lay together on the picnic rock, the pair of them. The balky sun and his pale, pale chest when he undid his shirt. Even then she heard the rattling inside. But that wasn't what stopped her. It was the thought of Ma's hands, those chapped fingers. The swell of Ma's stomach, the promise and the threat of another child, and the pies, the sheets, the roasts and gutted codfish, the tears, the spats, the mending—always something needing mending—these were the things that said, *Don't be stupid.*

Of course he took it another way.

"I'd be the happiest guy in the Dominion of Canada if you'd do me the honour of being my wife. Will you, Dolly? Till death do us part.

"I do love you," he repeated, when he needn't have. He needn't have at all.

The book's best section, in her opinion, is "Songs of Vagabondia." No need to consult the pages once the doctor's gone, reciting lines to herself and to the ceiling, which must be there. Bliss's purple asters in their autumn haze: she can see them. Tiny mauve stars, the signs of summer's end and fall's hastening, the last of the flowers to go. They bloomed by the cliff and in the hollow above the stony beach at the Point, where the fields and the spruce woods gave way to the lakes' shimmer.

Late that summer, at the tail end of August, she and Jimmy had rooted around on hands and knees, like pigs she later saw in Italy sniffing out truffles. A pair of golden chanterelles rewarded their trouble, almost too beautiful to take home and fry. He was awfully thin by then, and even after being outdoors his face looked waxy, pale as the candles Ma stocked up on for winter storms that brought down the wires.

But on that drippy day in June, offering no more than a shrug, she had picked up the flattest stone at her feet, shale pointed and fine as an arrowhead, and sent it skipping out over the lake the way her oldest brother had taught her.

"Who knows, Jimmy, what my plans will be? Where I'll be or what I'll be doing."

Her answer had more to do, finally, with Bliss's poems than it did with Ma. It had all to do with roaming—her feet, if not necessarily her heart. So it was Bliss who buttoned her lip against saying 'yes.'

Soon after finding the mushrooms he started coughing blood—and she was offered a spot in Normal school, quite unexpectedly. Her plans took shape almost too quickly by Labour Day.

"Abyssinia," she told him: her way of conscripting geography to make a point.

I'll be seeing ya.

"They called it the poet's disease," she wants to tell the nurse and whatever shapes, whatever sprites rise and dance from between the book's pages. Shelley, Keats, the Brontës, Elizabeth Browning.

They were going to read Mann's *Magic Mountain* too, she and Jimmy, but found its prose long and meandering, lacking in rhyme.

'Tomato juice is good for it, I hear,' Ma wrote in a letter, rather pointlessly, because by November he was in the san up in Kentville, and she up to her eyeballs in exams.

But in the shifting shapes—is it the light at the window? Leaves or cats or birds flocking past?—she thinks of Keats, his chilly room by the Spanish Steps, the light gone out of the Roman sky, and his narrow bed, his death mask. It was all there the time she travelled to see it. Poor Keats, and Bliss too—also dying alone, impoverished, cold. And Jimmy, gone by the time she came home, briefly, for one last Christmas there. Too late to change her mind and tell him yes.

Before the start of the holidays the tuberculosis took him.

The dead never fall out of love.

And now she sees him. The snow sifts down, replacing the leaves; yet their feet aren't cold. It melts into his coat, its soft heavy flakes, and he's holding something out. Not a promise, not an offer, but a present. The snow dissolves the paper and underneath it the gold-lettered cover warms her hands, its cloth a rich, fine-woven rust, not at all faded but new. Beware rust and moths, the minister always said, the one in the pulpit high above the furnace, not the one with the cat.

"Nice to see you, Dolly," he says, smiling. "Dolly-girl, this is for you."

POLIO BEACH

W E'RE OLDER NOW, MY COUSINS AND I—THE COUSINS WHO
would occupy my mind. A couple of us have children grown
up and far-flung, who themselves have little reason to come here. My
own reasons for coming dwindle steadily; by the end of this day they'll
have dwindled to none? But this bears no thinking of, just now. Taking
a beach break—a respite in the sad business of burying an old aunt, the
last of our mothers' family, and divvying up the 'spoils,' her worldly
goods—we walk in solitude, my husband and I. On this windy cres-
cent locked between cliffs, the furthest merging with the town of my
mother's birth and its slag heap's glacial outline, we walk to put in time
this dark July afternoon.

It could easily be mistaken for early spring, the sea a roiling
dark blue: whitecaps, breakers, bits of plastic bobbing on them. Spray
stings the air—with a foulness, we realize, as the dog noses the tide-
mark and a tilting sign anchored in concrete comes in view: *Warning.*

Outfall. A sludgy current froths, waves flinging murk onto the sand—ribbons of toilet paper, not kelp—this once-pristine beach where we swam as kids and my mother and her sisters before us. Abandoned, it's a floating landfill. The dog roots at the pink plastic of what could be a prosthesis—a doll's leg—then darts around a diaper, the detritus of people too busy stumbling through the days to cover their tracks. It's as if the sun-splashed shore in my memory never existed: scalding sand under untroubled feet and blankets weighted with stones, oranges, towels, shivering bodies. The only evidence of what was is a charred stretch of boardwalk passing a boggy oasis of alders, burnt wood littering the battered dune. Vandalism or some party's bonfire gone wild? This can't be the place we swam, can it? I call to my husband—but he's out of hearing, hastily leashing the dog, sidestepping something no doubt gross. It *can't* be the place. Yet it is, its ruin a large, fairly final nail in the lid of a chest of memories soon to be set adrift. Having come from Halifax, I'm missing home.

To everything there is a season. Still, feeling relief that, having quit coming here years ago, Aunt Flo was spared seeing her old shore "go to pot," I linger, longing to find something unchanged—evidence of finer days. And there it is: the brackish pond behind the fouled dunes, its stream emptying into the sea, the suck of its current so strong it still cuts the beach in two. Unbreachable now as then, it offers proof that the filthiest spot is indeed where we spent hot afternoons—hours of hen-rooster-chicken-duck—rewarded afterwards with Orange Crush from the crossroads' store, its dripping cooler. Wasn't life sweet, in the days when Ma cut oranges into dories—*Rory's in the dory, and he can't get out*—and sprinkled on the white death?

Turning my back on it, I take a last look at the nearest cliff, blunt sandstone that once glinted like a fat archie rolled in sugar—in my mind's eye, at least—and pick my way over the spray-pocked sand. Such are childhood's mirages, and the feelings that come, at a certain age, of having occupied some lost universe.

Black clouds meet the horizon. Spray beads the car's windshield and my husband flicks on the wipers; the engine throws off heat. The dog yawns, curling up on the back seat. It wasn't always so disgusting, I say, a feckless protest, and again the past seeps forward in dribs and drabs—as if it's dammed and its pouring out too fast would exhaust it, a reservoir emptying like the pond back there, where stories lie of this or that one drowning, learning to skate or swim, of the model boats my grandfather built and tested before anyone had cars. Isn't the past shaped of exactly these things?

"We used to say you'd catch polio from that stream," I tell my husband, smiling at how it brings what's lost to life. "It was so frigging cold, we believed it too—you believe anything when you're six, I guess."

Flo's little bungalow is as she left it: the living room with its floral upholstery, plants dropping leaves. How did we forget to water them, certain she'd return from hospital? "A bird that tough makes you think they'll last forever," says Gregory, her only nephew.

On the table lie the reception's leftovers: store-bought finger-foods, an extravagant Tim's cake which no one's had the nerve to cut—foods Flo herself would avoid, disliking chocolate and the prospect of sharing germs with a roomful of people: a staunch wielder of fork and knife, Flo. My cousin from away, Felicity, uncorks a bubbly white that Flo would've snubbed for a red.

"Thought I'd go all out," says Gregory, self-congratulatory, helping himself to a large slab of the cake, his doing. The last of our kin in the town, Gregory will miss Flo the most. So good of *you* to have stayed for her, the rest of us say—Felicity, Grete, also come from out of province, and I. Silently my husband drains his glass and leashes the dog for a walk, though rain begins to streak the windows.

Such good care you took of her, we agree—though it wasn't Gregory the hospital called with Flo's diagnosis or her passing, wondering about arrangements. His phone oddly, mysteriously out of range.

"You've had so much to deal with, Greg," repeats Grete, who, like Felicity, has always nursed a strange attachment to down-homers, the town itself no place you'd visit without good reason to, unlike the misty sea- and mountain-hugged villages north and west of here. Yet we came, as often and as faithfully as we could, staying close to Flo in ways we didn't, haven't, with each other.

"To Flo." Felicity raises her glass—one of our aunt's, a miniscule, crystal sherry glass in which even the chips are ladylike. Grete laughs, dangling hers, already emptied.

"God yes, to Flo!" booms Gregory, and Felicity busies herself topping everyone up. Her green, almond-shaped eyes already register the dust overtaking knick-knacks and pictures with names masking-taped to their undersides. Trinkets and tokens of a life of comings and goings in rising then weakening waves like radio signals, or rings on the pond's surface.

"Well, it's too bad she missed the summer."

"Loved a beach day, didn't she though."

"Damn rights—never gave a crap how cold it was, either."

"Just peel off, jump in, and give'r."

Maybe it's the wine, though I'm wondering where my husband's got to, keen to leave us to our grieving. Because I'm laughing and nod-ding, though the Flo I knew was not such a swimmer but a cautious breaststroker who hugged the shore, permed curls snug inside her bathing cap.

"She saved my life, you know," our cousin brags and Felicity and Grete snort—"Here we go"—recalling when we were kids and Gregory locked himself in a fridge. But he shakes his head, and I feel the echo of icy currents, the kind pale as stretch marks over the sea's calm. So the past comes back.

The scorching sun marooned his ma and mine and Flo on their blankets, while he and I plovered and hopscotched—the ocean too frigid for more than toe-dipping, cold enough to give a kid like me polio, teased Gregory, who knew how to swim. Since I didn't I was happy snuggling close to Ma, sucking on a Rory-dory while Aunt Glenna tugged up her suit and rolled over to bake. Throwing fistfuls of sand then dipping his blue plastic pail, Gregory threatened to fling it—*Polio, polio, who wants*

polio! A polio bomb! A joke? Ma gritted her teeth. Auntie Flo, who didn't have children, ducked under her towel.

Glenna's laugh switched to a shriek at Gregory's selective dousing. Why wasn't Ma jumping up to give her first aid? Take her temperature, hold her hand, give mouth-to-mouth resuscitation? The things a nurse did in a bad situation. Ma's smile was knotted; she rolled her eyes at Flo. I guessed what this could be about: Ma said polio was in the hospital, not the ocean; she should know, she had a friend who limped from catching it as a child. Vaccination was a word I knew from school. A drop of something pink on a sugar cube? A round scab on someone's upper arm, like a brand from a car's lighter, I speculated, having watched *Bonanza* and my aunts lighting cigarettes off one. What I also knew was that kids got sick, the children's hospital full of them in oversized cribs and iron lungs, kids in casts and in wheelchairs, on crutches and in leg braces: Ma said so.

"It's no joke," she said, her voice enough to put us in a cast— well, Gregory, who it was aimed at. "You never joke about disease." She glared so hard that silent Glenna scowled and drop-jawed Gregory. Gregory, who could do no wrong, grabbed his pail to refill it. "Don't," his ma said, and after a while the sisters leaned back watching the slow, glassy swells wash ashore, gulls bob, and a tiny white fishing boat haul nets—the sea a perfect blue thunder that rolled us with it. My small feet shaped waves in the sand, the light through my eyelids the red of a plastic bucket drying in the sun under that fixed, cloudless sky.

"Your mother could be a hardass, eh," Gregory says—a joke except for the way his eyes cross mine, this middle-aged, balding man who does caretaking for a living. "Some serious, wasn't she."

But that afternoon I remember her laughing, pointing down the beach to the stream glinting in the sun. "If you were going to catch anything," she said, "it'd be from there." Both her sisters, peeling back the flaps of their bathing caps after one last, futile attempt at a dip, nodded, Glenna adding that just that March a kid had almost died going through the pond's ice. For some sort of emphasis she slapped her quivering thighs, Ma shaking her head and Flo mimicking their complaints about orange-peel dimples, till Gregory, stabbing the sand with his plastic shovel, complained of thirst. Refusing Flo's Thermos of juice, he yelled for pop, then whined to go home. I zipped my lips, of course. It was Greg's way or the highway, Ma once said, nothing at Aunt Glenna's ran the way Ma ran things at home, like in a hospital—everything having its time and place—except in the case of the ashtray beside my uncle's chair and the bird that drank from a glass atop their TV, bobbing and dipping "till the cows come home," Glenna said.

"I could stay forever," my aunt moaned, a sand flea hopping from her girded stomach to Flo's knee.

"I-want-pop! Give-me-pop!" Gregory ranted louder and louder. "I'm dying here, I'm dyin'!" His feet squeaked, kicking sand. His fists pounded the blanket. Nestling closer to Ma, I clung to her neck. "Orange Crush, Oraaange Crussshhhh," Glenna mimicked the sea, shaking her head. "Give us five more minutes, Greg—you can do that, right? Just a little longer." Sighing, "Run off now. Just for a bit. See what you can find."

"You too, Marcie," Ma nudged me. "Keep him company—just for a sec." I knew that voice: it was for yet more catching up, never enough time to hear all about who'd died, gotten sick, or suffered other awful things since the sisters had last been together. Its impatience made me miss my dad in Halifax; he'd have taken my hand and run along too.

"See what treasures you find," coaxed Flo, the one who'd never married.

"I'll bet there's treasures—jewels," Ma said over Glenna's whisper, something-something about their other sister, the one they were missing, stuck in Ontario.

"Try thataway, maybe?" Ma waved us towards the spot good for finding beach glass, best of all the blue of VapoRub jars. "And pick some shore coal!" she called cheerfully. The three of them had already moved closer, Glenna sifting sand through her fingers: the sign of rapt attention.

"I don't agree with pop," I heard Ma say, squelching my sugary hopes. Gregory was out of earshot, tearing towards the stream. Its banks a proven trove of feathers and seashells and, once, a dried squid as papery as onionskin, the bead of one eye staring up.

Veering that way, dropping our buckets, we toed the hem of seafoam, felt the undertow grate our heels. "The frigger's a time machine!" Gregory yelped as the beach and the froth roared us backwards. Pebbles glittered. Gulls wheeled. My feet felt webbed and numb, my heart thumping as the waves dragged then shoved us back to dry sand.

"C'mon, bacteria," he called me, making a beeline now for the stream that swung and chiselled its way to the surf. Its banks caved under his giant, trouncing steps. "Josh-wah fought the battle of Jericho, Jericho, Jericho," he yelled tunelessly, stomping the dark sand as fast as the current could sweep it away. "And the walls come a-tumbling down!" I sang out, hanging back. Its gold glint deepened to the brown of cola; rank with eelgrass and mussel mud, it smelled brinier than the sea. "Is it poison?" I hollered, my question lost to his splashing.

Gingerly I parked my bum on its cool, sandy ledge. Light enough to sit without toppling it, I kicked my feet, watched the tickling yellowness glide over them. Whooping, Gregory scooped up armfuls of it, geysers flashing down over me. "Gonna be a cripple! Marcie the cripple! Won't be able to walk 'cause the polio'll take your legs off!"

It felt the same as when a wave had once knocked me under: the wanting to cry but being too scared to, the sting up my nose. From down the beach—far enough that her bathing cap looked white instead of pink, like the head of one of Flo's hatpins, not the dahlia it mimicked—Ma waved. Standing, Aunt Flo draped something over herself; shielding her eyes, she waved too. Gregory's ma was still pressed to the sand, so it really looked as if there were just Ma and Flo, Glenna no more than a beach bag or water wings without air. Then Ma lay down too, leaving only Flo sitting up. My cousin went on splashing and jeering, though his teasing eased into something gentler, brotherly—didn't they all say he was as good as a brother?

"Frig off—you won't get the polio. Don't cry." His sunburnt face darkened under the cruising shadow of a gull. "But you don't wanna know what's in the pond, bacteria." Sucking in his lips, he made a sombre, popping sound. A guy had drowned in there when our mothers were small, he said, and a kid too, late last winter, trying to skate.

Gregory had a habit of talking through his hat, Ma said.

With a wild yelp, he raced off when the sand under him let go—the ground in a cartoon earthquake. The yellow only came up to my frill, but next was quicksand—the stuff that buried people alive—pulling me downwards. The stream tickled my ribs as my cousin waded near its mouth. Filling his pail repeatedly, he flung the water back at itself, then dropped to his knees, digging feverishly. No matter how fast he scooped sand, the hole filled in. Distant laughter filtered down to us.

Gregory waded deeper and deeper, to where the yellowness thinned, buckling over itself in thick, fast wrinkles. As I sank deeper, I guessed that Ma and my aunts were having fun—and I still had legs and feet, the yellowness no different from peeing under water, a warming clamminess, as waves pushed closer. Their tingling cold swelled and slid away, swelled and slid.

Polio lived in hospitals.

But where was Gregory? Where had he got to? His pail twirled on the ripples, bouncing on the froth. As if buckets grow on trees, Ma would say—pop and chocolate bars too. Once, well out of Glenna's hearing, she'd called him spoiled. The thought of salty sweetness filled me, until a wave knocked me backwards, pushed bubbles up my nose. Through its gurgling thunder I heard myself howl. But I was okay, I was fine, crawling onto hot sand.

Out in the swells a bird was fishing—diving, sinking, beating the water with its wings—something I'd seen more times than Ma and them could shake a stick at, Gregory would say: nothing special, nothing to turn your head. Eating sandwiches Flo packed, all through lunch, over and over we'd watched flashes and bobs of white, tiny fish wriggling from beaks.

Now what I saw was a paleness—the paleness of curls?—as I squirmed against the grit caught in my suit. Everyone said Gregory had such pretty hair, what a sin being wasted on a boy, even Ma said. Next there was a scream—a squawk—as pale and scratchy as the sand, a sound rolling in and rolling out. Too, too far away to be a person, to be him.

It was Flo who twigged to it, Flo who'd glanced over as he ventured out swinging his bucket. Who'd seen the waves tighten around him and, who knows, when his feet left bottom. It was Flo who broke from a trot into a dash; Glenna peeling herself from the blanket, hurtling forward, Ma too—all three having removed their bathing caps, despairing of a swim. They were fully inflated water wings the way they skittered over the sand, wisps of it like smoke trailing them.

Somebody shrieked. Perhaps it was Flo, petite but full-bosomed, the oldest of the sisters, waves zooming around her and breaking as she plunged in. The water past her chest, she waved her arms over her head as if flagging someone down. A wave smashed over top of her, and another.

No matter how I squinted, no matter how I stared, I could no longer see Gregory, that bird. There was a shout, and there they were: Flo buoying a small flailing thing in her arms, sinking, bobbing, thrashing—Glenna frozen in the surf up to her neck. The noises she was making were like an animal's as Ma waded out, held onto her so the sea wouldn't take her too.

I'd seen the man earlier spreading out his towel below the dunes, taking off his shoes. Not noticing me he angled closer, flying past. Red bathing trunks. Dodging the stream, he jack-knifed under the place where yellowness fanned into blue. Slicing through waves, his arms chopped the sea. Glenna was screaming, screaming, screaming as he swam. The sea had moved the buoy that was Auntie Flo and my cousin farther and farther down the beach and out and out, so it wasn't hard to imagine them disappearing past the horizon like the fishing boat.

All I could do was close my eyes.

I remember the white string swinging from the man's trunks. I remember him carrying Gregory ashore, Flo staggering behind. I remember the man pushing on Gregory's chest and my cousin barfing water. My aunt Glenna lying on the sand crying, then kissing them both—and Flo sitting on the beach, her head between her knees.

"He could've killed the two of them," Ma whispered later, out of their hearing.

I remember that Gregory got to drink all the Orange Crush and eat all the Oh Henry! bars and Scotties chips he wanted. He was the king of the castle that night, the two of us allowed to stay up past bedtime to watch *Bonanza*—it went without saying.

I remember Flo bending to kiss my forehead, trembling but patting my cheek as if nothing had happened.

⌇ ⌇

"Flo said it herself, she'd thought we were goners. She told herself, 'Well, at least it'll be quick.'" Gregory rises stiffly, shakes out his legs, thick and white and still quite sturdy in his khaki shorts. He disappears to the kitchen for a minute—we think it's to find more wine—but when he comes back he has a long brown envelope in his hands, legal-size. "No time like the present—guess we should get to it." He is the executor, of course.

I hear my husband come in, the scrabble of wet paws, the leash being hung, a hush.

Felicity's eyes water. Grete holds a cherry tomato between her long fingers; she takes forever bringing it to her mouth.

"Ah, Flo always did like you best, Greg," Grete laughs wryly, glancing around as if waiting for a bottle—a magic one—to appear. But there's just the empty one and a vase with her name on the bottom, already noted.

"She decided to leave everything…well, what can I say, you know it's all here, right? She signed it all over."

The room goes silent.

"What was I gonna do?"

The well-kept house is a broken shell without Flo, we all know it, as is our shared past. From the kitchen there's just the sound of the dog licking herself and my husband trying to stay invisible.

"Yeah?" Grete's voice is harsher. Felicity looks stricken. Gregory natters now about power of attorney, responsibilities, doing his best.

"She saved my life, for fuck sake," he says, and then something unexpected: "Here's the thing. The house? I'm signing it over—youse can all do with it what you like. I'm outta here, I hope. Been thinking of McMurray, Red Deer, Nanaimo, what the hell. This way you'll have somewhere to come to—how she would've wanted it, really. The least I can do."

Grete folds her tomato, barely nibbled, into her serviette.

Felicity looks aghast.

My husband waits in the doorway. Nobody speaks; there's just the jingle of dog tags.

I picture Gregory boarding a plane, flying across the continent. It is easier to imagine the skeleton of a gull soaring over dry, dry land.

It is the least he can do, unload this place on, *unto*, us, and in some sort of bargain free himself.

"Sure," I finally say. Because it *is* the least and also the most, finally, this unburdening of shored up things lost, unsalvageable, their encumbrance no more ours than it ever was his.

This. This is what he holds out.

ACKNOWLEDGEMENTS

"The Race" was published previously in *Riddle Fence #20* (2015), and "Doves" in *Running the Whale's Back* (Goose Lane, 2013) and in *The Antigonish Review* (Spring 2005). "Solstice" was performed as part of the 2012 Lilah Kemp Reading Series at Bus Stop Theatre, Halifax. "The Vagabond Lover" first appeared in *Nova Scotia Love Stories* (Pottersfield, 2016) and "Polio Beach" in *Local Hero* (Breton Books, 2015). Many thanks to Beth Follett, Mark Harris, Andrew Atkinson, Richard Cumyn, Ronald Caplan, Lesley Choyce, and Corey Mombourquette for their input on these.

The Bliss Carman lines in "The Vagabond Lover" are from *Bliss Carman's Poems*, McClelland & Stewart, 1931 edition.

My deepest gratitude to my editor, Jaime Forsythe, and the wonderful crew at Nimbus, especially Whitney Moran and Terrilee Bulger, for publishing the collection. Thanks to Lorri Neilsen Glenn, Binnie Brennan, Ramona Lumpkin, and the friends to whom the book is dedicated, and, as always, to Bruce Erskine and our sons; to Garry Gilfoy for his stories about Doris, 1927 international swim marathon champion; and to Bess, in memoriam, for joyfully sharing her Bliss.